LOST ESTATES

Lost Estates

by

Mark Valentine

Swan River Press
Dublin, Ireland
MMXXIV

Lost Estates
by Mark Valentine

Published by
Swan River Press
at Æon House
Dublin, Ireland
in November MMXXIV

www.swanriverpress.ie
brian@swanriverpress.ie

Stories © Mark Valentine
This edition © Swan River Press

Cover design by Meggan Kehrli
from artwork by Jason Zerrillo.

Set in Garamond by Steve J. Shaw

Paperback Edition
ISBN 978-1-78380-782-6

Swan River Press published
a limited hardback edition of
Lost Estates in May 2024.

Contents

Lost Estates

A Chess Game at Michaelmas

The branch line from the seaside town took me at a thoughtful pace westwards through four or five little halts or lonely stations. It was early autumn, and there were hovering patches of mist still lingering in some of the hollows and higher places. The sun, which had not dispersed them, was now beginning to abandon the effort. Its faltering rays tarnished the horizon with the patina of old brass. The day was dwindling.

There were not all that many other people aboard. I had on my old greatcoat, which had stayed with me through some rough times, and I shrugged my shoulders up inside it towards its deep collar, against the chill, which the dusty radiators were unable to dispel. I liked the lulling rumble of the rather decrepit carriage and engine, and the slow passage of the landscape, which descended to the sea on one side, though this was more felt than seen, and rose up to dun coloured downs on the other. We came at last into my destination, the terminus, with a certain amount of sighing and clattering from the train, and from the passengers.

Stark white letters stood out from a black panel glooming beneath a lamppost, already lit. These announced our arrival at Abbotsbury. The guard called this out too, as if some of us might still be in doubt. I stepped off under an ornamented wooden canopy which seemed extravagant for such a modest place. The design of its fretwork put me in mind of pen nibs and made me think of my own two favourite fountain pens, which I always have with me. I moved my hand to my inside pocket and made sure they were there. I expected to need them quite a lot. Then I gave up my ticket and went out through the little wicket gate, past a sign advocating the pleasures of cocoa. The deep crimson ground of this tin plaque and its curling letters, which emanated into figurative fumes of steam, were soothing and I at once rather longed, as I was meant to, for a beaker of that chocolate drink, particularly as the cold was already beginning to seep through me. Still, the walk ahead would soon help to shake away most of that.

At a melancholy grove of fir trees the station approach forked and I stopped, put down my haversack (another old friend from former days) and consulted once again the letter, which I admit I had already read over several times on the train. "We are about five miles across country from here," it read, "but you will not mind the walk. There are some interesting monuments to see on the way and some good views. I've made out a rough map. But bring a compass in case." No, I didn't mind the walk: I had done as much as this, and more, quite often in my wanderings in pursuit of my studies. I hadn't bothered with the compass. The expiring sun was a sufficient sign. And so, following the route that Ivo Winterbourne had made out, I took the left turn towards the village.

A straggle of other passengers plodded in front of me and in this sort of loose parade we covered the half mile or so to the settlement itself. I passed a few outlying cottages of pale stone faintly illumined by the tired sunlight, their stiff thatch streaked with livid green moss. I caught the ancient tang of woodsmoke coming from their hearth fires and it filled me with a longing, though I could not quite say for what. Ahead, the great staunch tower of the church rose from the middle of the village, but that was not my way. I kept a sharp lookout for the narrow track to the north which I was to follow. It was not all that obvious, but I was soon convinced I had found the right one. The path pulled away from the decorous little settlement, rising steadily. My white breath coiled ahead of me as if minor genies were leading me onwards.

At first I enjoyed the briskness of the air and the tug at my calves after the fugginess and inaction of the train journey, but I soon began to feel the burden of my bag a bit and had to stop quite often to catch my breath. I took the opportunity to look back through the wan light at the cluster of Abbotsbury below and, as I got higher, beyond there, to the coast, dimly seen. It felt like an adventure to be out on the upland and not quite certain of my way, despite the sketch map, and yet there was also a part of me that might have rather put up at the inn, and enjoyed the chatter in the bar.

Still, it was kind of my host to invite me, a stranger he only knew through correspondence, to stay a few days, and I could hardly have found any reason not to, particularly since the initiative in asking about his house and its particular custom was mine. With what I soon came to understand was a characteristic diffidence, he had said, "We are not in the least grand, you know, and I am mostly here on my own, so you will have to take things as you find them and pitch in, but I expect you will be used to that, from what you say. And I promise I won't ask *you* to play. Unless, of course, you are the King in disguise, which I suppose is possible."

As the haul took its toll on me, I kept my gaze to the ground and was sometimes distracted by the shapes of flints that I kicked up under my boots. I knew they were nearly all natural, but some looked at first glance as if they had been worked, and not into any practical use, as of arrowhead or axe, but into a kind of idol or godling. The shiny black facets seemed able to catch whatever there was of the diminishing light and a few times I stooped to pick one up and regard it more closely. I was tempted even to take one or two with me, but there was not much room in my bag among my clothes and books and papers: and in any case I did not think I quite cared to put them there.

Even though the track was mostly clearly defined and there were few paths leading away from it, I became a bit less sure about where I was going until I came to the summit of the slope I was climbing, which opened out into a long ridge. And from here, Winterbourne had said, I should bear north west along the crest until I came to the first of the monuments he mentioned, The Old Mare and Her Foals, which he had marked "Ancient burial chamber", and then, with what I supposed was an obscure hint of humour, "Do not linger."

It was difficult to see from the shapes of the stones why they might ever have been supposed to resemble horses. I did not imagine that even with weathering from the sea winds and the rain they had changed form very much over the centuries. The most that could be said was that they had that aspect sometimes seen in horses of seeming to stare at the horizon, as if wondering whether they ought to canter off towards it one day, not stopping until they found it. The way the stones leant forward, almost with a lunge, suggested a similar sort of attitude. They looked more like hunting dogs "at point" than horses. As I had been advised, whether light-heartedly or otherwise, I did not, however, linger, but carried on along the ridge, which now began a gentle descent.

The grey chalk of dusk was now being drawn across the day, and though I could still see well enough, I felt a distinct change come over the country I was traversing. It was hard to say exactly what this was, but the downs seemed more subdued, hushed, quite silent. It was as if the terrain itself was conscious of the watchfulness of the stones' stare: and I was also aware of being regarded in my progress. There was a moment, as I walked, when the sense gradually came upon me that I had passed into a different sort of space, a pause in the usual order of things. It was only momentary, and I can hardly explain it any better than that, but for a few paces I seemed not to be simply treading a worn path over the hills but passing through a haze of ashy motes. I stopped, and made myself do simple, practical things: I adjusted my haversack, crouched and retied a boot-lace, stood up and looked about me again. The illusion, if that is what it was, had passed, yet the impression lingered with me.

I continued the attempt to be busy, by looking again at my instructions. The next way-mark on the map was a stone circle, but it had a note against it: "Sometimes hard to see. Don't look too hard. Just keep going west." I thought that might have been more happily phrased, but I did as I was bid. The reason for the difficulty soon became apparent, because these were not standing stones rising prominently to about mortal height or more, but had fallen (or been lowered?) upon the ground. And in fact the grass had been allowed to grow all over them, as if it was thought better for them to be covered up. The effect, however, was rather as if some pack of grey preying creatures had concealed itself in the undergrowth, waiting with infinite patience for the right moment. As with the stone "horses", I had a distinct sense of watchfulness. But the downward slope lightened my steps and I strode resolutely onwards. It could not be so very far now, I thought.

At about half way down the long descent to the valley, the way joined a more definite track now heading due north again and this I gladly took, feeling once again much more assured of the route. This, I saw, would drop down to a bridge over the river, the Bride, and from there to the village of Long Bredon: but I was not to go quite so far, because before the little settlement was reached, I must turn away and follow, at last, the path to the house I was seeking.

The river, when I came upon it, was still quite a young bride, and, I thought, as I stopped to look upon it from the parapet of the bridge, a rather sombre one in the half-light of the dusk. The dark glinting of its ripples was like the black edges of the flints I had seen, and coldness rose up from its murmuring waters. A short way beyond this, "Look out for the lodge," Winterbourne had written, "and turn in there." This proved to be a small, thatched, octagonal building with gothic windows, its walls rendered in a sort of rhubarb-pink, vivid even in the dim of the day. The flaring red of a post-box on the opposite corner of the drive, and some rusting iron gates in a sort of ancient silver added to the somewhat peculiar palette. The gates were jammed open against tussocks of weeds and one of them sagged like some old retainer who can no longer stand upright but is determined to keep doing his duty so far as he can. I set off up the track.

The house was called "Brydian", and there had been a place here since at least medieval times and possibly further back, but the present building was, I knew, more recent. I had looked it up in county guides when I was trying to find out more about its particular custom. It was not, by country house standards, all that large, although certainly far grander than anything I had ever known in my upbringing or that of most of my friends and colleagues.

As I approached, I saw that it did not stand full square at the end of the approach, but at a slight angle from a bend in the road, and that it seemed to crouch behind rather wild outgrowths of climbers and creepers.

In appearance it suggested the symmetry and classical proportions of the late Georgian, but there were craggy touches and flourishes that suggested the influence of the nascent Gothic Revival. The effect was curious, like a doll's house refashioned by a follower of Poe. Nor was the approach dominated by any haughty portico or elevated terrace, but there was simply a tall gate in a wall of friable brick. Its ironwork creaked like a rook's call when I pushed it open. The way to the house was along a path of uneven grey slabs that resembled scales on some antediluvian creature's back. It led through the remains of an ornamental garden. In the grey light I paused to look at this. There was something alluring in its shabby decay.

The garden was full of topiary, which grew to slightly above my own height, and seemed indeed to be about to topple over. It had clearly once been fashioned into shapes resembling chess pieces, in tribute to the custom associated with the house, a neat enough if rather predictable gesture. But each of the leafy columns had now become overgrown: and some attempts to restore them had not been wholly successful, so that the green-work now appeared to depict peculiar figures. The rooks were no longer battlemented towers but hunch-shouldered ogres wearing lopsided coronets. The pawns were like stunted children, the bishops seemed to be tipsy, and the horses' heads of the knights looked more like jackals. As for the king and queen, their stately eminence had descended so that they had the appearance of crumbling monuments decked in verdant mummery. The effect was sorry, yet at the same time it had a sort of eerie accomplishment to it, as if some modern artist had decided to recast the chess figures into a new, apocalyptic form, denoting chaos and decay.

I was still staring at these green effigies when I heard light footsteps and turned back towards the house. A young man was approaching. I had an impression of a pale, sharp-featured face, topped by a bristle of dark hair that looked almost as indifferently cut as the topiary. He wore a mustard-coloured high-necked jumper and maroon corduroy slacks.

"You have made quite good time," he called. "I am glad you have found us. My map was good enough, then?"

I assured him it was, and made my unnecessary introductions. He insisted on relieving me of my haversack, even though I privately thought I was more capable of carrying it than his own rather brittle form. We walked in together up a few shallow steps—"Watch that one, it gives, rather," he warned me—and into an entrance hall that struck colder than it was outside. It was mostly empty. He deposited my bag beneath a hat stand which held a beret, a straw hat that had the appearance of being half-eaten, and a black umbrella sagging from its ribs like some decrepit giant bat.

"We'll eat in the kitchen," he said, "if you don't mind. Easier. And warmer."

He led the way along a stone-flagged passage that might have been a continuation of the garden path, and we emerged into a large warm room with a worn table in its middle. There was a great stove and he busied himself with the kettle and an enormous pan, from which emerged in due course a very hearty vegetable stew. I found I was hungry after my long journey and the walk, and enjoyed the rich savour of the broth. My host, I noticed, ate rather less, and was assiduous in replenishing my bowl, but when I protested that he should have more too, he said he'd had quite sufficient.

During the meal we made rather tentative conversation: about the late war, of course, and the rationing (food was always a topic for conversation in those days), and the garden, which had yielded most of what we had eaten. He said he was glad I enjoyed it, as that was pretty much all he had to offer, and it would be our staple fare. I assured him of my enthusiasm. After we had eaten, we retraced our steps and he took me through a door leading from the hall, into a high-paned room where a reluctant fire glowered in the grate. I had the sense that this chamber was not used all that often and deduced that probably my host used the kitchen as a sort of all-round den, when he did not have visitors.

"I'll get some coffee," he said, as he showed me in. "It'll be chicory, I'm afraid. All we can get these days."

I murmured polite appreciation again and while waiting for his return scanned the bookshelves, a thing I can never resist doing whenever I find myself among other people's books. They were mostly, as I expected, sturdy county histories and the bound proceedings of local learned societies, acquired no doubt because it was thought the right kind of thing to do rather than because of any particular interest in their contents. Military history, agriculture and the memoirs of faded statesmen were also well represented. Slightly more surprising were a few shelves of medieval history, mythology and some slim volumes with titles evoking the elements, and indeed the elementals, which I supposed to be emanations from the shades of the Celtic Twilight. I wondered if these represented the selections of some unexpectedly aesthetic scion of the line, or possibly those of my host himself.

"Tell me a little more about your studies," he said, as he returned, bearing a tray. There was a hint of emphasis on "your", as if he were implying that I had indeed glimpsed his. "I'm interested. You said that ours is not the only—or even, I think you mentioned, the oddest—of the customs you've discovered. I'd like to know more."

"Well, first," I returned, "I'd like to hear from you exactly your own understanding of the custom here. The house is full of symbols of it, but would you confirm just what it is?"

He stared at me for a few moments from his dark eyes, which seemed to draw the strongest contrast from his pallid skin.

"I am sure you already have it right," he said. "In one sense it is quite simple. We hold this manor from the King in return for a service or duty if you prefer. In fact, I believe the exact term is that it is a form of serjeanty. I told them when we had a squad billeted here. 'Watch out,' I said, 'I'm a sergeant of the King, you know.' "

"What did they say to that?"

A faint smile crossed his rather wintry features.

"I believe they remarked something to the effect that they had quite enough, ahumm, *blessed* sergeants already, thank you."

I joined in his gentle humour.

"And the service that you must perform is?"

"Ah. Rather unusual. Should the King ever visit, we must be ready to play at chess, and we must count all the pieces from the set at the end of the game and place them safely in their pouch. And that's it. Isn't it odd? Can you think of an explanation?"

"Has your family never had one? I'd like to hear your own views about what it means."

He shook his head. "No, I don't think they thought much about it really. And, well, you know, I'm only here rather indirectly. Sort of cadet branch. Gosh, first a sergeant, now a cadet. And yet I'm not in the least military! But no, I never heard any ideas about the thing. Most of them weren't terribly interested, I believe, and the others saw it on roughly the same level as a fête."

"A fate? What, you mean a sort of doom upon the house?"

He laughed again, but his splutters turned into a fit of coughing.

"No, no. A village fête. I mean the kind of thing you have to do because it's expected, even though it's a bit of a nuisance. Although I *have* sometimes wondered if it might be the other sort of fate too. I've talked to Dee sometimes about one or two ideas."

I didn't like to ask directly who Dee was, but I was curious, and he saw me struggling with this nicety and, after a pause, relented.

"Dee is Cordelia, really, but I'm allowed to call her Dee. She lives up the road, at the lodge. Makes a sort of living making astrological pot-pourri, bespoke. We're friends. We must get her to do some for you while you're here."

I nodded, though the offer did not kindle much enthusiasm.

"Well," I said, "you asked for any explanations for your custom here. I can think of two, but neither is quite satisfactory. You know, I'm sure, that just about the only type of tenure most people might have heard of is the peppercorn rent. Those really do exist, by the way, I've got quite a list of them in my survey so far. The notion behind these is that there needs to be some form of payment to make the whole thing legally binding, but that nobody really wants any money to change hands, and so they settle for something purely token. For some reason, and we don't quite know why or when, the form for this sort of agreement came to be the 'payment' of three peppercorns. It is usually three, though there are variations."

I stopped, because I could sense myself beginning a lecture. Winterbourne, however, seemed genuinely curious, or else politely convincing.

"Yes, I see. But now, how does that fit with what we have here?"

"Only that your form of 'rent' for the manor is just as nominal, isn't it? It only ever falls due if the King visits here and wants a game of chess. It's just a picturesque way of saying, in effect, nothing to pay. It was always assumed, probably, that the visit and the game would never happen. And indeed has the King ever visited?"

He hesitated and looked away. His gaze seemed to stray to the book shelves, as if he were thinking of something he had read there. Then he smiled and tilted his head slightly.

"No, never. I do follow your reasoning, and yet it still doesn't quite explain why we have this particular form, and not just, say, the three peppercorns."

"It doesn't get us very far, I admit. I do have another idea, but it might seem far-fetched."

"Go on."

"Suppose it is a sort of code, shared and understood between the King and your ancestor . . . "

"Distant . . . " he mumbled.

" . . . and although the service talked about counting chessmen and making sure they are kept in order, it really meant something else. Keep an eye on the barons in their castles, the bishops in their palaces, the knights gallivanting around the country, keep an eye even on my queen and the people I use as my pawns."

"Gosh! Sort of secret service role, you mean? How thrilling."

"Yes, exactly so. It would be a private role, expressed sardonically in the form of the chess pieces."

"Do you know, I'm quite attracted to the idea. So now I'm a sergeant, a cadet and a secret agent. It's very, um, imaginative of you. Who'd have thought it?"

I wasn't quite sure if this last remark was a tribute to the originality of the idea or a reflection on the unexpectedness of it, coming from me. I rather suspected the ambiguity was intentional.

"And do you really believe that?" he queried.

"It's no more than a possibility. But can you tell me any more about the custom?"

"Not very much. But I should add that a few—what shall we call them?—elaborations have grown up around the original matter. For example, we do have our own particular chess board and men here, and it looks and, well, feels quite old. And I gather that my predecessors have always been most particular about counting all the pieces and putting them away properly whenever it was played amongst ourselves, even though that is really nothing to do with the duty to the throne. But another thing is, that what we play isn't proper chess, exactly."

I wasn't quite sure what he meant by this.

"You mean, it's not sort of championship level?"

"No, I don't mean that. I just mean the proper game itself, the usual rules. No, what we play here is different, in several ways. That's not all that unusual, I gather. We have quite a few books on chess in the library, as you can imagine, and I've been idling the time away by looking at them. I haven't quite got used to being a, well, gentleman of leisure. It seems it was quite a while before the rules of the game were finally formalised. There are records of quite distinct versions before then, often thought to have exotic origins—Persian, Byzantine, Moorish and so on.

And ours must be a relic of one of those, or something similar."

I found this "elaboration" of the custom at once interesting, and said so.

"May I see it, while I am here?"

He looked at me steadily for a few moments, then looked away again to the door, and back again.

"I am sure you will," he replied, hesitantly, and I thought that this was not quite definite permission.

"It may cast some light upon the custom," I said, "and in fact, yes, I have encountered these sort of additions to original customs elsewhere also. It's part of a way—isn't it?—of enjoying the tradition. Celebrating it, cherishing it, you might say."

"I suppose so," he agreed. "You think us fortunate, don't you, to have such a quaint thing?"

I noticed that although he had told me he lived here almost alone, and I had certainly seen no-one else, he always spoke of "us", meaning, I assumed, the line to which he was heir, the house of his family, even if his own link to it was, as he had said, distant.

"Well, yes, I do," I replied, "it seems to me quite delightful, for anyone interested in history or legend."

"You might think so," he said, and repeated, "you might think so," and I had the sense that he was going to say why it might not be quite so charming as I supposed, but he allowed his words to fall away, and diverted the conversation.

"But do tell me all about these other instances. You promised you would, you know. I really know quite nothing about manorial customs, apart from ours. And not much about that."

"Just a moment," I said, and went into the hall, which struck even colder after the warmth of the kitchen and even the slight glow of the fire I had just left. I reached into my bag and took out the long and stout book I had brought with me.

"This is my bible and my atlas," I explained, as I rejoined my host. "I hope you'll enjoy the title."

He took it from me, holding it carefully in his delicate fingers, and turned the first few pages with elaborate patience. When he came to the title page, he read out the main heading.

"*Tenures of Land & Customs of Manors Originally Collected by Thomas Blount and Republished with Large Additions and Improvements in 1784 and 1815*, newly edited by William Carew Hazlitt," he recited and added, with a smile, "Goodness, what a fanfaronade! And are we in here?" He turned to the back, found the index, looked up his house, and then consulted the relevant entry, running his fingers down the page. "Well, I feel as if I passed the exam, you know. Wasn't my answer pretty much spot on?"

"Yes, indeed," I assured him.

But he was reading on, and looking slightly preoccupied. Then he sighed, shook his head, and handed the book back to me.

"You know, we've never really known which king it was. And I see he doesn't either. There's talk, of course, of Richard the Lionheart, then of his brother bad King John (not so bad as all that, I've sometimes thought) and then of the infant Henry III, which means I suppose really in practice some Regent or Constable or somebody."

"Again, that's not unusual," I reassured him, for he seemed quite bothered by the point, "records from so long ago are fragmentary and we really rely on chance survivals. An oral tradition is sometimes all there is. But, as to which king it was, well of course that doesn't affect the obligation which, after all, is to the Crown, whosoever wears it."

"Yes. Whichever king it is . . . " he agreed, though he still seemed doubtful. I felt I was not quite fulfilling my duties as a guest, and so decided to lighten his mood by talking about some of the other customs, similar in kind.

"I have to say to you, sire, that you really got off quite lightly, you know. There is an account in here of a tenancy held—not from the throne—on payment of a snowball at Midsummer and a red rose at Christmas. How would you like that?"

A light briefly danced in his dark eyes. I was glad to see it, although later, when I remembered his gaze, I thought of the glint in the dark facets of the flints I had seen on my journey.

"That's very poetic. What can it possibly have meant?"

"Well, I'm afraid Mr. Carew Hazlitt has a rather hard-headed explanation. He says that since these rents were obviously impossible to fulfil, it simply meant that the tenant and the landlord would meet and agree some *other* fee each year. It was just a way of regularly reviewing what that payment would be."

"Oh, no, surely not," he riposted, quite aghast. "It seems much too elaborate for that. No, I won't believe it."

"Well, neither does he, quite. And he does add that he has seen pockets of snow lingering in the high fells near the place in question even in June: and that a rose may be preserved by artful means."

"Even then, he is being a little too literal, don't you think? No, I have always had the feeling that there is something else behind our rather picturesque duty here, and now I feel the same about this one. Are there any more? I can quite see why you have made these the object of your studies."

I was glad I had caught his imagination.

"There are many. Some, like yours, concern a personal service to the King. For example, there is one where they must, if the monarch should be in the county of Lincoln at Christmas, and if he so requests, process before him bearing a white wand. Like yours, I don't think there is any record of this actually being required, but it's a pleasant image. And there is even one which requires the subject to maintain strumpets for the King's use in a certain town."

"For ceremonial purposes, no doubt? As a fanfare?"

I burst out laughing.

"You could call it that. Strumpets," I repeated, emphasising the sibilant beginning.

"No, really?" He joined in my amusement, and for a moment some sort of pale rose came into his cheeks.

I nodded.

"They were bawdier days then. But in fact there are quite a few families that do have to keep a trumpet." I puffed out my cheeks and twiddled my fingers to show that I did now mean the brass instrument. "Or rather, to be more exact, a cornet or a horn. Their duty is to sound it to warn of the coming of the king's enemies. Some of them have very beautifully chased, ornate examples."

"Do you know, I think I have heard of something of the sort? It rather reminds one, doesn't it, of 'the horns of Elfland faintly blowing'."

He became thoughtful again. I began to flick through the, to me, well-known pages of the extensive treatise, and to tell him of a few other curious manorial customs I had found there. To each of these he gave some appropriate response, but I could see that his attention was now really elsewhere and, after a while, our conversation began to falter into hollow silences. At length, Winterbourne rose from his chair, stifled a yawn, and said he would show me to my room. The old polished wood of the newel posts on the stairs, at the bottom and top and where they turned, I noticed, were carved as chess figures. Like the topiary, they seemed misshapen, perhaps worn by the years or possibly battered about when the house had been requisitioned.

The windows looked out onto the garden. Clouds drifted across the moon, and from above the topiary, in this shifting play of shadow and silver light, seemed quite uncanny. The evergreen figures flickered as if they were about to move. I watched for some moments because I really had the impression that they must, at some sudden turn of the lunar light, wrench up from their roots and stride across the paving slabs. But the dark cloud-wrack began to thicken and the fitful rays of light to become fewer until, as I continued to gaze out, the carved yew effigies became still, solemn black columns.

In the morning we made a simple breakfast of tea with thick rough chunks of toast smeared with honey. My host, I thought, was a little more taciturn, as if slightly wary of having said too much to me the previous evening. I decided to ask him about less speculative aspects of his inheritance.

"Have you ever tried to find out what the official position is regarding your tenancy?" I asked, "I hope you don't think I'm being intrusive?"

He looked at me in a rather startled way at first, then busied himself with tidying up the cups and plates.

"Oh, no, not at all. Yes, when I first came here, I thought I ought to try to put things on some sort of firmer footing. But I didn't quite know how to go about it, and the family solicitor wasn't a lot of help. In fact, he said it was all better left unsaid. But in the end I did write a rather tentative note to the Treasury. They seemed the right sort of people."

"Did you get a reply?"

He smiled rather wanly. "Oh, yes. It was a masterpiece of official evasion. It intimated that they had no record whatever of any pecuniary transaction relating to the property, in their interest: and it was not entered upon any register of national assets, so they did not consider it necessary to pursue any claim in this regard: nevertheless they reserved the right to do so if the matter should prove to be otherwise, and so on, and therefore it would be advisable for any persons concerned to maintain such records as they thought appropriate. I gathered from this that they hadn't really got a clue what I was asking about."

"That's not all unusual," I explained. "Most of the ancient tenancies I've looked into are only a matter of custom and have no real documentary grounding. In some cases, in fact, the particular talisman is almost itself the proof—an engraved horn, or a pepper pot, and so on. Perhaps that is the case with your chess set?"

He nodded, but did not rise to this hint at my interest in the board and pieces. I decided to try another line of enquiry.

"With the houses that have horns to warn of the King's enemies, it's usually clear from their locations why this might be the custom. They are near the coast or on old borderlands, or in remote locations—forests or marshes. Do you think anything of the same kind might apply here?"

Winterbourne looked at me in an abstracted sort of way for a few moments.

"It might be so," he said. "We aren't all that far from the coast, after all, and we're in a sort of gap in the downs which might have had some tactical importance, I suppose. The country around here is full of ancient remains, as you've seen. But if you want to know more about where we are, you'll do better to go and talk to Dee. She has been here much longer than me, though we're about the same age. She lived in the lodge with her aunt, you see, well before this place came to me. It was her aunt who started the, er, the mystical pot-pourri business, and Dee has just kept it on. I've told her I have a visitor, so she won't be surprised. Of course, she might have 'seen' you anyhow." He smiled. I saw that this was his tactful way of bringing our conversation to a close, for the present. He seemed preoccupied, and I guessed he had other things calling his attention. I thanked him and said I would call on her straightaway.

I walked back along the drive to the lodge, with its Gothicky windows. There was no chimney-smoke, though the day was quite cool. The door stood slightly ajar. I patted on it but there was no reply and even though my touch was light it swung further open. It gave directly onto a large room dominated by a broad old table. This was strewn with a big pair of haberdashers' scissors, a gnarled roll of string, sheets of brown wrapping-paper, cotton pouches and curled-up little scrolls of paper. Despite some qualms, I stepped further in. Delicate, elusive scents entered my breath, and all around the walls hung bunches of drying herbs, in which even I could make out lavender and thyme, but there were others I did not know. As I stood there, still hesitant, I thought that I had entered a scene from some old Dutch master—the herbalist's cottage, as it might be, and that all that was lacking was the simply dressed human figure, full of grace, intent on their task.

"Who dares enter Madame Tarragon's domain?" demanded a robust voice behind me. I turned too quickly, and almost knocked from her hands a tray of fresh cuttings. The young woman was about as far removed from the vision I had conjured as possible. For one thing, her hair looked as if it had been cut by the same brusque methods as the topiary, and for another she wore a baggy jumper of flaring scarlet quite unlike the duns and ochres of the oil paintings.

All this, of course, I took in at a single embarrassed glance or so: and I dare say she was making up her mind about me too, although no doubt with rather less interest.

"Um, I'm visiting Brydian," I said, and introduced myself.

"Yes," she replied. "I know. Madame Tarragon is my trade name, by the way." She gestured at the contents of the table. "I sell herbs by post. And enchantments. Well, bits of good advice, really. But people like to think of them more romantically. And why not, if it helps?"

I admired this practical approach.

"Do you like it?" I asked.

"I suppose so," she replied. "My aunt was the original, you see. She taught me all 'bout the herbs, and what to say to people, and then left it to me. It seems to work all right, I suppose. Keeps the wolf from the door and all that, although sometimes he's getting close, prowling around the garden you might say."

"Winterbourne says you know the country here very well," I began.

"Oh does he? Well, I suppose I do. I use it for inspiration. Helps with the work. Clears the brain a bit. It was my aunt who really knew it well, of course. She thought this place was right for her work, it had lots of little nooks and crannies where she could gather things."

"I see. I walked from the train over the downs. I saw the Old Mare and so on. Ancient terrain, isn't it?"

"Hmm, yes. Did you manage to clear up his mysterious tradition for him? The stuff about the King and the chessboard?"

"Not exactly. But I suggested a couple of ideas, and I told him about some similar customs."

"What, also involving chess?"

"No. There's nothing quite like that."

"I dare say not. He frets about it a bit, you know."

"Does he? Why?"

"Well, I suppose he's quite new to it, really. Distant scion and all that. I expect he told you that."

I nodded.

"He thinks he's missing something, you see," she went on. "About the story."

"And is he?"

"Very likely. I expect we all are. I have some ideas, but I'm not sure. You know they call this part of the valley The Gap? Between the two sets of downs, you see. Must have been an important route once, I suppose. Into or out of—well, wherever," she finished, then added, with what I thought was a distinct swerve of subject, "What are you like with parcels? Never been my strong point. Strange collision between object and wrapping paper more like. Sit down there, and as I pass you the things, you do 'em up."

I did my best to comply. There were a few examples of her work already in a basket and I saw what she meant. They looked like wrinkled pixies. I endeavoured to make mine slightly more presentable and she nodded approvingly. For a while we worked in silence punctuated only by practical observations about the work in hand, and then, as we got into a sort of swing about the packing, I asked how well she had known the family at the house.

"The people before," she began, then tailed off, before resuming somewhat cautiously, "quite remote cousins, you see, didn't pay any attention to this chess business at all. The old Major was a lovely fellow but not what you'd call imaginative. It was just his house and that was that.

Of course, he knew all about it, but it didn't interest him. Might not have been a bad way of looking at it either. I believe he did get a letter once or twice from somebody or other, like you, following up quaint customs, but he never replied. Or so I gathered."

"I can quite understand," I said, as my fingers continued their tussles with the sheets of wrapping paper and skeins of string, "I've had a certain amount of short shrift too. On the other hand, other houses have been glad to tell me all about it, often with—er, well, embellishments."

"So I imagine. Well, you've come at the right time, as it happens. Today being Michaelmas. It's one of the quarter days, of course, when rents fall due. So who knows if the King might come?"

I paused in my packing activity.

"Michaelmas?" I repeated, in surprise. "But no, surely—that was some days ago. Thirtieth of September."

"Not here, me deario. Here we celebrate Old Michaelmas, of course. The *proper* time, before they mucked about with the calendar. So it's always in what more foolish mortals call the second week of October."

"I see," I said, "yes, I've heard something of the sort elsewhere. And does, um, anything in particular happen on Old Michaelmas here?"

"Nothing at all, before" said Madame Tarragon, succinctly. "But Ivo has other ideas, I think. Well, we've about finished here. Not too bad at all neither. Do you fancy a job? Sorcerer's apprentice? Moderate remuneration. Good fortune always in your hands. No? Can't say I blame you. Well, let's go up to the house and find out whether the King has turned up yet."

We came upon Ivo Winterbourne in the garden, where he was just finishing clipping the yew topiary. The shapes did not look any more like they should than before, even if they were somewhat severer in outline. He nodded to us, and we joined in, by collecting up the clippings and taking them to a heap in a corner. Ivo then swept the cracked paving slabs with meticulous care.

As we waited for him to finish, my gaze drifted around the little enclosure, and in an angle of the old brick wall by the entrance gate, within the twisted shade of the green columns, I noticed a rusting ornamental wrought-iron table with chairs placed on either side of it: and on the table top I could see the black and white pattern of a chess board. I looked at the herbalist and saw that she had noticed it too. We exchanged glances and, as Ivo returned to us from his final tidying-up, he said, noticing our interest, "Yes. I'm going to bring the pieces out soon, too. It seems the right thing to do. Just to sort of honour the custom, you see. In case the King should come." And he smiled rather bashfully at us. We both murmured appreciation of the idea. Then we went in and took lunch.

After the meal, we went into the room I thought of as his study, or library, where we had discussed the custom the evening before. Winterbourne seemed hesitant. He went to the window and gazed out at the garden. The day was already pale and there was a hissing in the trees from the beginnings of a rising wind. I wondered if he was having second thoughts about his proposed little ritual. But then he turned to us.

"I wonder if you'd mind—I thought, at first at least, I'd like to sit out there on my own for a bit. Just to sort of think about things. Come and join me a bit later."

We hastened to assure him we quite understood. As we left, I saw him go to a carved aumbry in a corner of the room. From outside in the corridor I heard the creak of hinges infrequently used. We made our way to the kitchen, and stoked up the stove fire against the chilliness that seemed to have come upon us. I busied myself with my notes, while Cordelia drew a crumpled notebook from a pocket and seemed to be casting some accounts, with much furrowing of the brow. The warmth began to steal through my limbs, but I was aware still that beyond the radius of the fire's glow there was a distinct cold. Every so often, when I looked up, I saw the young herbalist gazing abstractedly, her worn fingers working a pattern to themselves, and sometimes even her lips murmuring. The figures must be very tough indeed, I thought.

I must have drowsed for a while under the soothing influence of the fire because when I came to, my notes had scattered on the floor, and the embers had sunk low. I hastily got to my feet, gathered up my papers, added some small coal to the fire and stirred it up hopefully with the little iron poker. Of my companion there was no sign. I stretched and wondered if I should go in search of her. Then there was a bustle in the passage beyond, and she came in from the kitchen garden, bearing in her hand a sort of small garland of green herbs that she had woven together. I recognised from the scent the sharp tang of rosemary, but it was mingled with other elusive savours I could not quite place. The keen wind seemed to come in after her. She nodded to me but did not utter a word, and made her way to the front of the house, into the hall and through the great entrance door. I followed her and as I did so it felt as though I was joining in a sort of procession, even though there was only the two of us; it was the way she strode, solemnly and carefully.

We emerged into the walled garden and were at once buffeted by the strong breeze. I wondered why on earth Winterbourne was still sitting out there and thought it was carrying a somewhat whimsical devotion to the ancient custom, as he interpreted it, rather zealously. But there he certainly was, seated at the chess board in an alcove of the wall by the gate, his hair ruffled by the wind and indeed even his body and limbs seeming to ripple as it passed across him. The two of us paused, uncertain whether to approach nearer. We stood there watching for some time. I could sense Cordelia shifting slightly, as if about to go over to him, but each time deciding against.

Then a strong gust thrust its way through the garden, rattling a watering can and bucket and bending the yew columns backwards and forwards. I was distracted by the noise and the sudden movement and did not at first notice the effect on the chess player in the corner. But when I returned my gaze to him, I drew in my breath sharply. The pale shadows of the topiary figures seemed to be flickering over him so that their shapes worked across his face and figure. Their odd, newly-cut angles cast their silhouettes on his still form: and as they did so, I saw him raise his white fingers and move a piece upon the board. It blended in with his fingers so that I could hardly see where these ended and the piece began, there was a blur between them.

I thought at first that he was simply taking hold of it, trying to stop the figure toppling and rolling in the wind, but then I saw that he had definitely placed the piece beyond the opening squares. Without reasoning to myself, I at once looked opposite him. The black side was in a deeper shadow and I could not make out if there was another figure there, but as another gust coursed through the garden it seemed to me that one of the dark pieces was indeed moved as well. Winterbourne's face was full of fierce concentration and I found myself wondering if his high, hard regard upon the board was itself the cause of the movement of the pieces, as if he could have willed them to move.

The yew topiary continued its wild waving to and fro and as I switched my stare between its contorted movements and the pieces on the board I saw that they were the same shapes. It was not, I now understood, that the green columns were raggedly-crafted approximations of the usual chess figures, but that they were faithful simulacra of the pieces on this board, which were like no other I had ever seen. And those pieces were still being moved, swiftly, by two sets of fingers, the slender pale fingers of the young scion of the house, and some other dark hand I could not fully discern: but as those shadowed pieces moved, I thought I saw a glinting that was like that of the black facets of the flints I had glimpsed on the hill track before. But still I was not quite sure what I was seeing.

Indeed, the writhing of the yews and the ripple of the wind again caused the pieces on the board to look as though they moved of their own accord. I watched them, transfixed, and as I stared, their shapes seemed to take something of the ancient forms of the stones I had seen on the crest of the downs as I had walked there the evening before. I shook my head and tried to dismiss this idea, but it still clung to me. The carved pieces seemed drawn from the very terrain itself. I found I wanted to shout out at Winterbourne, to ask in some futile way whether he was all right, but my mouth was stopped because the deep dank rank smell of the yews, raised by the wind raking through their sombre limbs, was filling all my breath. And all the while, as I held myself against the succession of strong gusts, and switched my gaze from the topiary to the board and back again, the movements of the game seemed to go on at a great pace, one piece hovering and descending quickly after another. I was unable to follow the course of the play because it was so fast and because the yew shadows flickered over the board, but I was filled with a strong sense that it was being pursued fiercely, and the continual rising of the wind brought with it a keen sense of great peril, as if it was goading the players on. Again, I wanted to call out to Winterbourne, but felt my tongue clogged by the bitter miasma of the yews.

And then I felt rather than saw Cordelia sway and move beside me and lunge towards the player, or players, at their game. As she did so, I saw one of the two tallest figures among the pale pieces, a shape that had a stark crown upon its head, rise up and then return emphatically to the board. There was a shudder in the air, followed by a pause, a heavy sudden silence. No sooner had it slammed down on its chosen square, than Cordelia, with deft fingers, encircled it with the wreath of herbs she had woven, and stepped swiftly back.

"Checkmate," she whispered.

At once a particularly violent gale of air tore through the garden and flung up the heap of leaves and twigs that had been cut from the yew bushes that morning, just as if some great arms had thrust themselves underneath the pile and thrown them up high, with a vast malice. They seemed to stay suspended for a few impossible seconds before the spiked tongues and little claws first flew from each other and then were drawn back in together: and as they were sucked back they began to form a haggard, jagged shape, a great figure comprised of darkest evergreen and utter black, an absolute, ancient essence. Then there came to me the phrase, I could not say from where, *The Yew King*. The stark form existed, stayed in place, for what must have been only a few moments, but which seemed to me to like a void in time, where it was all that could be known, or ever would be known. Then all its parts scattered and clattered to the ground and were whirled about into a green chaos.

Beneath the whirling of the wind I could hear Winterbourne's voice counting. "Two white hounds," I heard him say, "two black hounds. Two white jesters: two black jesters." And as he recited these, I saw the pieces disappear from his fingers into a drawstring pouch whose mouth gaped open to receive them. The counting went on until he came at last to the royal figure that had ended the game. "And one white queen. With garland," he added, looking thoughtfully across to Cordelia.

❋

Ivo Winterbourne regarded us both keenly. His face was still pale but I thought I saw a new vigour in its sharp features, and his dark eyes gleamed.

"I don't know what you both saw," he said, "and the truth is I don't know what I saw either. I can't say for sure if there was something opposite me moving the black pieces, or if my fingers were moving both sides. I really can't. I just seemed to be swept up into a sort of trance. But one thing I am sure about. That was a true game, a tough game, and it seemed to me played for the highest ends. Not just for the house, I mean . . . " He let his thoughts wander back to the fraught, feverish match he had seemed to be playing against some strange opponent.

We had gathered in the kitchen and had just set aside our finished bowls of thick soup. The deep aroma from the pan, and the crackling of the stove fire, were both comforting.

"When I came here," he resumed, "it seemed to me that the place was falling apart a bit, and had been for some time. There were good solid reasons for that, of course. Everyone's having a hard time, I know that. But I wanted to make myself a proper custodian, a steward if you like.

I began to think about the terms on which the house was held, which on the one hand seemed so fanciful, and yet were also quite definite and specific. My predecessors, of course, ignored all that completely." He smiled briefly. "I can't say I altogether blame them . . .

"Nobody could say exactly which English king it was that had bestowed the manor upon us, and there was no real record of it whatever. Yet it was a very old custom. So I began to wonder if there was some other explanation. Perhaps, I thought, if one went back far enough, it all began with some particular local king: Saxon, even Celtic. So I started looking into what was known about that. And I gradually became convinced I was on the right lines, but I still couldn't quite get hold of what it all meant. It was the pieces themselves that gave me the best clue, I think. When I first looked at the set, I couldn't make them out at all. I thought at first they were just rather odd interpretations of the usual set. But they aren't that. No: they are all part of the King's entourage, you see. His giants (the rooks), his jesters (the bishops), his hounds (the knights) and his dwarves (the pawns). They are all there, in the old mythology. Only the queen is unchanged, although she is rather special . . . and unlike them, *she* is not his."

He glanced across at the young herbalist. She was twining a stalk of some long herb around her fingers.

"But they all suggested a particular kind of domain, and not an earthly one at that. So I decided on my little ceremony and then—how does it go? 'Enter the King of Fairies at one door, with his train.' And not only King of the Fairies either, but also King of the Underworld. I never saw his face," he added, quietly.

I told him of the phrase "The Yew King" that had come to me, and he nodded. "Another of his names, I am sure."

"What will you do now?" I asked. "It must be tempting, for all their history, just to burn those pieces."

"I know it. But I cannot do it. And I do not think it would make any difference to what is due. Besides, we have paid our rent. The King has come, the game has been played, the pieces have been counted, and they have been put away again. I don't know how time works there, nobody does, except that it isn't at all like ours. It may be that we have quitted ourselves for many generations to come. But do you know—"

He turned to me. "I really think I might have preferred 'a snowball at Midsummer and a red rose at Christmas'."

Worse Things Than Serpents

I remember once in the depths of Norfolk coming to a crossroads with a patch of green on which stood the usual black and white signpost. Well: I knew where I had come from, and I knew, in a certain sense, where I was going, which was straight ahead. But this junction offered two other options. The right arm read "Church"; the left offered "Garden". There was a half-deflated blue balloon attached to this arm.

Norfolk churches are usually worth stopping for, so I drove up the unmade track to the flint-knapped tower. It was one of those churches that are nowhere near any settlement. Either the places it had once served had long ago gone, or there had never been any, and it had been sited here for some inscrutable reason. It stood in a slight, gentle rise, surrounded by elder and hawthorn. There was no notice-board by its narrow iron wicket gate. The arched door was unlocked and I entered into a dusty silence.

There were points of interest, certainly: some past parson had collected fragments of medieval glass, which had been mounted in an abstract order in some of the windows, so that they were like mosaics of light: and the sunlight playing through the bright colours played on the floor of the nave. I stood looking at this stone kaleidoscope for some time. In their own way the abstract colours had a spiritual quality at least as potent as any saintly or angelic figure. The effect put me in mind of the flowers I might see in the left hand option, the garden, so after a little while I returned to the crossroads and took that direction next.

But as I went on, there was no sign of any garden: not only no second notice indicating a way in, but nothing that looked in the least like it might be the destination. I drove on much further than was strictly needed to establish that there was no garden, and I began to get the curious idea that by choosing the church I had lost the garden. It seemed all at once almost a consequential, indeed a metaphysical, choice. I turned around and resumed my original route. The garden that was not there remained in my thoughts, of course, as the perfect paragon of a garden, not just in its blooms and ornaments, but in its serenity and seclusion. And the shrivelled balloon now also seemed a harbinger, of joy withdrawn. But no doubt it was just that the sign was old, and the garden no longer open.

Still, I was on the alert whenever I saw one of those homemade roadside notices painted in irregular letters on carboard or wood, though they usually offered eggs, honey, or jam. And my attention was rewarded when I noticed one with an even better temptation: books. To be precise, it read "Brazen Serpent Books", in white paint, but the elements had done their work and it was now rather smeared. Either as a joke or through lack of forethought, the final "S" slithered away from the rest of the letters.

The trade name was not, strangely enough, unfamiliar to me, for I had once studied seventeenth century printing, when I was researching early almanacs, and recognised this as the emblem of a publisher who had set up his sign "hard by St. Swithin's Yard". There were many similar such, often involving fabulous devices, just like inn signs: The Gilded Lyon; The Black Swan; The Unicorn; The Green Dragon; The Elephant; The Phoenix.

I was at this stage on a secondary road that cut across heathland. I was in no particular hurry, my destination was less than an hour away, and I wasn't meeting anyone. My time was my own. There had been a settlement of sorts about ten minutes back, not much more than a small congregation of cottages around a brick chapel, and I thought there was not another cluster of black cubes on the map for some miles yet.

Mindful of having missed the garden, I did not want to miss the bookshop. I followed the sign into a narrow lane which twisted and turned for some time. I half-expected to find that the bookshop, like the garden, was mythical. But just as I was beginning to think about finding some gateway to turn around in and return, a further sign appeared. It had been knocked askew and now pointed up to the sky, and a third soon followed. It indicated into a broad corrugated iron shed, painted at no very recent date in a dim black, now streaked with encrustations of rust, white damp and verdigris. I supposed it had once been a wayside garage or workshop: there was a wide dusty forecourt. I drew up.

The shed had a bell outside with a cord underneath. I gave it a clang. No-one emerged, so, after some hesitation, I went inside. It was dimly lit from two dusty windows, and I could not see a light switch, but there were books all right, albeit only a few crooked shelves of warped, blistered wood. I had a quick glance around in case there was anyone in the shadows at the back: this is not, after all, uncommon with the more reclusive or temperamental booksellers, who do not like to be disturbed. But there was nobody there. Evidently, they had left it to itself: perhaps it was an "honesty bookshop". I had known a few of those, including one in Presteigne, where I had found a rare Sally Purcell pamphlet, *The Devil's Dancing Hour*, and there were also boxes of used envelopes to unusual correspondents with obscure professions or industries.

I went back to the entrance, blinked in the light, and looked about. The yard was empty and silent. Well, after all, the signs had urged me here, so there could hardly be complaints of intrusion. I started peering at the books nearest the door, where there was a bit more light. The first one I picked up was an improving Religious Truth Society book, and next to it was a translation of it into Italian, *Il Serpente di Bronzo*, c. 1860. Next to that was a sacred poem by Harriet Cope of 1827, also about the serpent. Then there was an annotated edition of John Horne of Lynn's *The Brazen Serpent; or, God's Grand-Design* of 1673; a treatise on *The Brazen Serpent as a Symbol of Life Eternal* by Erskine of Linlathen, 1879; a book of sermons of 1820 on a similar theme; a long poem, ditto, "which obtained the Seatonian Prize", by Handley Carr Glyn Moule of 1873; *The Brazen Serpent Lifted Up on High* by Richard Farnworth, circa 1666, in a new rebinding in crimson, with the eponymous serpent limned in gold; and, in a handmade wallet, a printer's device of the serpent of c. 1599, the serpent facing left, a very choice item. And here was a French study from the 1920s, *Un véritable Serpent depuis des siècles*, and *La Vera Serpento*, which seemed from the incidental matter to be a work in Esperanto.

I cast my glance a bit further afield. The titles were all variations on the same theme. There were some Fiery Serpents, and some Serpents Held High, and some Serpents in the Desert, and one or two Ancient Serpents. There was even, and here I thought the collection was kicking its heels up a bit, a book on the musical instrument called the Serpent, although the illustrations of it didn't make it look much different to the idols in the other books. Well, you could hardly deny that the shop did what it said on the wayside signs. When it said "Brazen Serpent Books", it meant just that. It wasn't, after all, the only narrow specialism I had come across in my collecting journeys. In the New Forest there had been a dealer in Antarctic Philately, in Saffron Walden a specialist in croquet, and in the Forest of Bowland a leading authority on books about Nepal and Sikkim, with an occasional adventurous lunge into Bhutan. Indeed, one of my own acquaintances, John Wroth, specialised in Coptic, Abyssinian, and Mozarabic manuscripts. I had idly thought about issuing imaginary catalogues of even more recondite subjects, but I suspected there would still be takers.

And I now rather felt the call of the arcane subject here. Until then I had never had any notable interest in the symbol of the Brazen Serpent. I might have passed just such titles by when I searched the shelves of theology looking for stray titles that had got in there by mistake: *On Strange Altars* by Paul Jordan-Smith, actually about book-collecting; *Mystic Voices* by Roger Pater, which admittedly sounded as if it belonged there, but was in fact a book of ghost stories. But now I found this collection curiously interesting, and decided I wanted to have at least one of the titles, if only as a souvenir of a singular bookshop. Was there anywhere to pay? I went further in again. On the far wall was another of the hand-made signs, this one just a black arrow pointing downwards, and on the worn, wobbly table beneath was a collection box. A stylised serpent's head had been carved into the polished chest, while the grains and knotholes of the desk were used in such a way as to suggest scales. The box gave a slight suggestion that here was the chapel of some mystic sect and in a way perhaps it was. In fact, some sort of long black cape hanging on a stand in the corner added to the impression, for its folds suggested a soutane or cassock, though doubtless it was just a waterproof.

But which book to get? I didn't much fancy the Religious Truth Society one. I had once been a customer of a corner bookshop in a little market town run by a very pious and kindly old lady, Mrs. Manifold, and she had lots of these. They all had brightly coloured covers with embellishments of gilt and silver, because they had been aimed at the Sunday School prize market. I commented on this, and Mrs. Manifold agreed they made a nice display, but added, "And so *improving* too." I had not quite thought of them in that way, and although I respected the sentiment, I did not regard it as an extra allurement. Nor did I, casting my gaze over the shelves in the shed, feel drawn to the long Victorian verses or homilies. The foreign language books sounded more exotic and would look well on my shelves, although it would be more trouble to read them. The antiquarian works had the advantage of rarity and age but would presumably—I hadn't yet looked—be priced accordingly.

No, what I wanted was a volume which of course followed the theme here, but was also in my usual areas of interest: the decadents of the Eighteen Nineties, interwar fantastic literature, the occult and esoteric, obscure modernist texts. Admittedly I didn't actually know of any in those spheres which addressed the Brazen Serpent, but that was rather the point: could there possibly be some unknown work of that kind? I turned again to the shelves, and began to go through the books again. There were rather more French texts as I advanced, and I thought it possible some might be by forgotten symbolists or surrealists, but I did not know enough to be sure.

And then the order, if there was any order, took a sudden swerve and we were back among apocalyptic literature. These had vivid titles and cover designs and if all else failed one might do just as a curio, so I continued flicking through, and then I came to a sudden halt; a name had caught my attention. It adorned a pamphlet with lilac paper covers which had rather erratic titling, of the sort where the lettering appears to be adorned with thorns. Even so, the author's name was still tolerably clear. It read: "Louis Horne", and the title, which was a characteristic one for him, was *The Serpent, The Serpent!* I turned the brittle pages with care, trying to contain my eagerness: there were long columns of verse, all equally fond of the exclamation mark. But these, unlike the more solemn volumes I had seen earlier, I would be very glad to read. For he was a seer.

Louis Horne, the younger brother of an artistic and literary family, had been the wildest and strangest of them all, and was apt to entertain visitors with long incantations upon the Book of Revelation, which some at least agreed had a certain power. This was perhaps in the same style. I had never heard of it, and of course I had to have it. I went gently back to the title page. There was a pencilled note there, but in the growing gloom I could not make it out. I took the little booklet outside into what was becoming dusk, but at least the light was a little better. As I stood in the forecourt there was a creaking sound from the rear of the shed, and I looked towards it. Perhaps there was, after all, someone about. That at least would save me from trying to decipher the price. But no figure emerged, and I soon saw the cause of the creaking. At the far end of the edifice there was a weather vane. I hadn't noticed it before because I was intent on getting in to the books. It was, naturally enough, in the form of a serpent rampant, coiled around the pole of the vane. At some point it must have been gilded, because I caught glints of light as it swivelled slightly in the wind. I watched it for a few moments, and by some curious effect of the wan light and the gathering shadow its tongue seemed to flicker. I was tempted to put mine out too, but desisted.

The vane was not uninteresting: I had once acquired in Stamford one Christmas Eve a little scarlet pocket-book of Norfolk weathervanes, and very diverting it was too. But the Louis Horne opuscule was the thing just at the moment. I squinted again at the faded pencil scribble. The first character, larger than the rest, was evidently the bookshop's emblem, and it was very like the weather vane. I glanced in turn at the two. Yes, the shape, and the coils, and the tongue, the same. But what was the price? It was getting late and I wanted to pay and get away. And then puzzlement and dismay came over me. There was no obvious figure, and the inscription itself I simply could not make out. The characters hardly seemed to belong to our alphabet. There were echoes of our letters, certainly, but these were faint, and they did not make up any recognisable word. Well, perhaps this was some cryptic trade jargon: I had heard that the apparently random jumble of letters seen on the front free endpapers of some books actually disguised a valuation code, or something of that sort. Perhaps the price was elsewhere. I looked through the preliminaries: nothing. I scrutinised the back cover and the inside back cover. There was nothing that looked like a price. I pondered. Just in case it might be relevant later, I copied out the inscription in my notebook, as best as I could.

What should I do? I could leave the find here, well hidden, and come back when there might be someone in the shop. I could make a generous guess at the price and leave that. Or what if I just put in a note explaining I wanted the book and had taken it with me and would be willing to pay their price? A bit risky, but most dealers are fair and would not take advantage of the offer. I went back inside and took the dozen or so paces to the back, now in deep gloom. I put the pamphlet down on the desk, took out my browser's notebook with a pencil attached and wrote out my message: "Serpent, Serpent! (Horne). Not Sure of Price", I wrote, "Happy to Pay What is Due". Then I added my details, tore off the leaf and stuffed it under a corner of the box, protruding a bit, where it would, I hoped more easily be seen.

The wind was getting up outside. It sighed through the shelves with a whistling, whispering noise. I almost thought I could hear the words *Serpent, Serpent!* repeated, over and over again. The iron walls muttered. The tails of the black waterproof stirred, caught in a draught. I heard a sound like a croak or a cough. Perhaps someone had arrived to close up? In that case, I could settle my business now. I strode quickly to the door, past all those books of the Brazen Serpent in their rows in the darkness. But it was the door itself making the noise, swaying on its ill-oiled hinges.

I stood in the entrance and looked out. Above, the weather vane was gyrating and grating again, this time with a repeated screech. I stared up at its dark silhouette. The wind was obviously veering about, and this had the uncanny effect of making the serpent seem to lunge, as if it had sighted a prey. I half expected to see it fly free of its moorings and take off into the twilight. I remembered that in the ancient text the original Brazen Serpent was to be raised up so that all the natural serpents of the wilderness should be summoned to it, and no longer be enemies of the chosen ones. There were several allegorical interpretations of this, of course, and as the books gathered here showed, there were certainly those who thought the Serpent might be raised up again. I shook my head. This would not do. I must resume my journey.

At least the rising wind refreshed my face as I stepped outside. I drank in the enlivened air. Dust swirled around my feet. I hastened to the car, and clambered in. Then I realised I hadn't after all got the booklet. Muttering, I went back into the shop. There was no light at all from the windows now, they were just panes of black, and the entire interior was fully dark, so dark that it was as if the shelves were not there. I proceeded cautiously down what I supposed to be the middle of the room, but I must have veered off, and found myself bumping into the hat-stand, knocking my forehead on one of the projecting prongs. I reeled back, clutching at the stand, and found myself grappling with the dark cape. For a few flustered moments I felt I was fighting it, until I righted the wobbling stand, and pushed the cloak back on to it. I stood, a bit dazed from the dash on the forehead and, despite myself, laughed. Unfortunately, some effect of the metal walls made an echo of laughter back at me, which was to say the least disconcerting. It didn't help that in my fleeting dizziness I thought I saw the serpent carved on the collection box stir. Of course, it was just the blurring of my eyes, and when I looked again it was quite still. Still slightly giddy, my thoughts wandered a bit and I recalled that snakes stop still when they are about to strike. I held my breath and backed away a bit.

Right above me now I could hear the serpent vane shrieking, and all around the corrugated iron walls creaked and scraped in sympathy. One of the panels, free of its rivets, flapped inward, exposing a narrow crack through which the wind billowed, adding its own hollow howling. I recovered my wits, swayed to the desk, and began patting the scaly surface, my fingers seeking *Serpent, Serpent!* It wasn't there. I felt all over the surface again, getting the strange sensation that I was touching a sleek hide. Still nothing.

The wind must have seized it. I dropped to my knees and crawled around on the floor: surely it could not have gone far. I found a fair amount of grit and dust, and even put my palm in some damp slime, but the feel of the paper covers did not come to me. As I lumbered about, patting and peering, my hand moved into emptiness and I almost over-balanced. I paused. There must be some sort of gap in the flagstones of the floor. Could it have got in there? Cautiously, I reached further in, but did not find any base. I felt further around, but could not work out where the edges were. I supposed it must have been some sort of inspection pit when the place had been a workshop. There were gusts of air swirling around the hole too, but they were far from fresh: in fact, they smelt pretty dank. It ought to be cleaned out and covered up, I thought, with indignation. What if my find had got down there? This was hopeless. I scrambled up and almost missed my footing into the hole: I was still a bit dazed, I suppose. It was as if the wind down there was pulling me in, and there was a hollow moaning. In useless desperation, I called out the title: "*Serpent, Serpent!*" I almost added, "Where are you?", but that sounded too much like a call from a children's game. The vane above my head gave more shrill shouts on its axle, as if in answer. I heaved myself back from the hole.

After fumbling about a bit more, I went all over the desk once again, the scales seeming to meld themselves to my hands, but it wasn't there. I lit a match (I had no torch), but the brief burst of flame did not last long: the wind maliciously extinguished it and several others I tried. With a burst of impatience, I seized my note from under the box, crumpled it up into my pocket, and stamped out to the door. The darkness and the narrow twisting lanes as I drove away forced me to calm down and concentrate.

❃

I told of this encounter to John Wroth, the ancient manuscripts man, next time we met, thinking that he might know all about Brazen Serpent Books, as there were some aspects that bordered his own field. He didn't, but in the course of my account I had shown him the inscription I had copied into my note-book. When I had finished the tale, he asked to see it again, and studied it for some time. His lean, rather narrow face became clouded, and he began to make notes. The fine pen he used formed shapes not dissimilar to the ones I thought I had seen. He tried out several, gazing at them, and pondering.

Then he said, in a casual sort of tone, "You did get your, er, promissory note back?"

I assured him I had.

"Just as well," he said, thoughtfully. "I'm not sure you would have been 'happy to pay what is due', you know."

"Oh, you've figured out the price!" I exclaimed. "Pretty steep?"

"Much too high," he said gravely. Then he smiled "Do you remember the old Mellstock church band in Hardy's *Under the Greenwood Tree*? Most churches had them of one sort or another until the new fad for organs and harmoniums came along. The parsons thought they'd be a lot less trouble than a band, but then they didn't know the ways of organists. Well, the Mellstock band are discussing the virtues of the various instruments. Strings is best, they think, they admire a drum, and they'll admit a bit of woodwind. Even that old black bass device that some find a bit peculiar. Maybe it is, to look at. 'Yet,' says Mr. Penny, 'there's worse things than serpents'."

And he wouldn't say any more.

Even so, for a lost Louis Horne, I do sometimes wonder. Perhaps it's as well I haven't been out that way again.

Fortunes Told: Fresh Samphire

"Most of Britain is marshland . . . "   – Herodian

"Even today Britain is still spell-bound by magic"

– Pliny the Elder

Some say the Phoenicians came to these isles long ago in ships with golden hawk-winged sails, and in niches on the shore left beads of sardonyx, blue ceramics, nutmeg husks, and strange gods. Some say the ships came from farther beyond, from the ports of Babylon, from the coasts of Mesopotamia.

Some say the oracles are consulted still, in the cliff-side harbours and sheltered coves where they read the litany of the seas and winds. You can still discern the signs if you trace your fingers in verdigris, or touch the pale lips of ghostly fuchsias. Monkshood gloves beckon at doorways and in ancient courtyards granite slabs bear letters that we can no longer read.

Whether all this is so, I do not know. There is old star-magic here, but it is not all. Others study the red and gold of well-thumbed playing cards. They have heard of queens with serpent faces playing sea kings of phosphorescent silver at cribbage, with wreck-wood boards and cards of coral and gold. The jester that is sought is not to be found.

There is a young man here who says the moon is made of sealing wax, impressed by the signet, twisted with beasts, of the queen of the stars, on her orders for the astrologers. Never look, O Crabbe, he says, at the Moon in Her Plenitude, full face on. I met him in the café here, drinking bitter tea from a black beaker, with grimaces, this boy, in a slate-blue shirt with white and purple irises, his ears curled like conches. He has seen, he says, two rose-red lions at the door of Mark. Sometimes he seems to have the wild bright eyes of merry-go-round horses.

In the street, a slim black racing dog is a streak of ink, writing in the rain. With the brief white flower of the yew, ravens build nests, foxes mate, the bruised clouds are black-blue. To the west, a lighted train is travelling over the marshes towards the grey sea, the sea that is sifting the sands in its ceaseless search. The sun is as slow as honey. The windows glint like silver visiting-card trays. A broken piano is playing in a luminous room above. The lost cabbalistic studies of Charles-Valentin Alkan, perhaps, from winged fingers. Beneath, the tired, crumpled parcel-paper faces of the passers-by are briefly uplifted.

There are voices in the garden. Lord serpent and the moss boy, iridescent, faintly green. The lions are among us, under the black planet's shadows. Bronze-purple glass. The lichen is writing in slow curled signatures. There are red beasts in the hills. The yew is sighing a secret bloom.

Crabbe. (I place my name here so I will remember. Much else I have forgotten, it seems.)

Crabbe has vanished, and yet he is still here. At the samphire shed. The roof was once thatched with dried reeds, but that has been replaced by corrugated iron, now marked with streaks of ochre and white crusts of salt. The walls are made of big slabs like altar stones. The place had originally been made as a shelter for those who collected samphire, "dreadful trade" as Edgar calls it in *King Lear*, because it is hard to find, and harder still to harvest, often in the teeth of the sea winds. There are still some who come looking for it for their own use, or to sell on a trestle table by the wayside. I once saw a painted caravan in a lay-by with a hand-daubed sign reading: "Fortunes Told: Fresh Samphire", which seemed a pleasing dual enticement. I sometime fancy that the keen dank aroma of the samphire still lingers about the walls here.

I have plenty of time for fanciful thoughts because the place stands so alone. And they are a way of forgetting about why I am here. I am here because my friend has, apparently, disappeared.

This wasn't discovered, if you can "discover" an absence, for some days. He never had much in the way of deliveries or post and he had always kept to himself. But after a while the few people who knew him began to wonder what had become of him, and one of them raised the alert. He always kept his door unlocked, so the local policeman knocked, called, then walked in. The place was as neatly kept as always, there were cold ashes in the grate, a plate and cup neatly stacked by the sink, an old pipe on the shelf above the fireplace, and the key was still by the clock on the bookcase, though this had stopped ticking. There was no note on the table, nor anywhere else.

A slightly hesitant, dutiful and careful search through his papers had turned up a will. It was not recent: it had been made some years before. It named me as his executor and principal beneficiary. He hadn't told me this—that was characteristic, he was always reticent about personal matters—but it didn't surprise me. I knew he had no near relations, and we had known each other since childhood. The will had led the authorities to me. They were reassuring, diffident almost.

They wanted to know what I thought might have happened, but I could not be of help. Perhaps, they said, he might have gone on holiday on a sudden whim, or been called to some urgent business. After all, people were free to come and go as they pleased. Could he have gone away, forgetting to tell anyone? I did not think it was likely: he was always considerate, and in any case I thought he was well-settled here. What, they then asked me tentatively, was his state of mind like? As to that, again I could not really answer: I had not seen him for some time. He always had a speculative turn of mind, I said. Speculative, repeated the constable, and wrote it down. He probably thought I was being polite. I suspect the only speculating he ever did was on horses.

And so the matter was left open and unresolved. There was nothing, strictly speaking, to resolve. There were no signs of "trouble", as the police officer rather vaguely put it. We did not speak of the obvious inference, that he had got lost on the sands and been overtaken by the waves. But his photograph was circulated to the local fishermen, coast guards, yacht-owners, and harbour-masters, and he was added to the list of missing persons. For some years he would now remain in a legal limbo unless and until I applied to have this made more definite. This I am in no hurry to do.

I had only a hazy idea of what Crabbe was up to, but I knew he was a keen observer of the tides and the skies, the grey birds and the tough grasses of this lonely stretch of coast. He could have become preoccupied by his studies and failed to return before the tide came in, though this didn't seem like him. Besides, he had other studies, and how could I know where they might have led him?

There is a riven shaving mirror over the primitive stone sink here. I look into it cautiously in case it has given up its power to reflect. But I am still there: my watchful stare, my thin stubble like drizzle. For a moment I wondered. As if a mirror might be blurred, as if its face of ice could be disturbed, as if, in place of its cold clear stare, the mirror preferred not to show what was there. Perhaps once, when he was here, it could not be sure whether what it saw it should faithfully show, or implacably disown, so it might never be known. The image was withheld, but it is still somewhere within. This idea has come to me only out of loneliness, I know. There is not much more I can do here.

The grain is shifting. The ancient slate creaking. There are wild nests of no known bird. In the brooding eastern skies beasts blossom. The black tea astrologer in the bitter wind is sifting thin green cards. Blue clouds of wax ink. Skeins dark as curled jokers. Grape-bloom signatures of mist, and black lions. A table, his cup, drinking deep. Plenitude.

The two irises.

A winged dog, couched strangers, a secret mate. The travelling twisted room, winter roses. A stone piano. Pale birds. The western marshes. Crows, black honey. The boy with the ears like conches, yew eyed. Her icy signet.

There is a corridor and at the end of the corridor a glass door and through the glass door another corridor. And outside no outside to be seen, a green film of smeared shapes on the thick glass. Walk, don't hurry, the doors will always be there, and the corridors will not disappear. The outside will not come near. It is not there.

The qualities of the palace of Gwyn ap Nudd are these, that it is never the same for whoever shall enter it. Nor is the door-keeper the same. Nor is the watchword the same. The boy taught me all this. I call him "the boy", because he looks so young. But I think he is really very old.

Crabbe

I stayed here with Crabbe once or twice, and he showed me an old track leading back into the marshes, a raised causeway. It wasn't obvious at first, you had to know it was there. We were up early, when it was still gloomy. At dawn's end we stood on a bare knoll, gazing at the horizon. The pale parchment of the sky had been illuminated by glowing scarlet, gold and copper, and we had watched for a while in some wonder, despite the brittle chill in the air.

As the light grew upon the dun and wan green land, his keen stare quartered the scene. The long, rounded mound we had made our viewpoint was the highest ground for miles around, though it would scarcely pass for a foothill elsewhere in the country. We had climbed to it along a slow, sinuous ridge, on this puddled track that glinted dankly where we trod. It might have been the samphire sellers who told him about it, and where it went. The "mouchers" they are called. But I think they give themselves another name. They still sell the salt stalks from door to door, tied with a sprig of sea lavender "for luck".

I remember on that walk he began to pay particular attention to where the hard white light of the emerging sun had begun to show more of the surrounding terrain. Pointing, he asked: "What do you see?"

I looked. "Turned earth," I said, "in big clods. Birch trees, a bit crooked. A stream, or a channel, quite wide, looking sedgy and slimy. Tussocks of yellowy grass. Some crabby dark trees, bare, are they elders? That's, I suppose, about all. Why?"

"Well, what don't you see?"

I sighed and my breath formed a spout of white spirals. "Well, I don't quite see why we're here, for one thing."

He exuded a dry laugh.

"Well, there aren't any houses, are there?" he pointed out. "How often can you look as far as the eye can see and find no house whatever, not even a remote farm-house? Very seldom, in England anyway. But follow this ridge from here east to the dawn and there's nothing. Not a dykesman's cottage, not a fishing lodge, not a thing. Why is that?"

"It's too wet to build on," I said, practically. But, of course, he had another theory. That there aren't any houses because no-one would be so foolish as to put one on this route. And I suppose he might not have gone out to the sea after all, as they all supposed. He might have followed the track one morning, as far as it would take him.

❊

The sifting sea. The signet. The yew astrologers on dark hills. A boy. Old photographs, like tarot cards, odd, hard to read. Little cobwebs. Sunlight shifting in black nests. Wild beasts. Red writing. The signatures. White blossom. Slow tea. Grey marshes. Blue-black clouds. The secret, luminescent dark. Lithe black dog, an elegant fountain pen writing in the rain.

Crabbe

❈

The sadness of belongings that no longer belong. Too personal to give away, too personal to throw away. So they sit, on the shelf, or in the drawer, as if waiting. Waiting for some other fate. His pipe, still with the faint indentations of his teeth. His clock, which I haven't brought myself to wind up, in case the time it stopped might be a clue. His cup and plate, still patient. The jacket on the peg behind the door, sagging without him. The whole room, I suppose, this cabin of sea-light and shadows, this place that sometimes seems to be not quite there.

❈

I can remember salt in the air. Sometimes it still seems to be there, when the wind is from the west. I taste it on my tongue. Then for just an instant it is as if I might flicker into a different sphere, maybe one I have known, maybe one I have never known before, I can't be sure. I feel I could let go and be gone, and wake in some other place, which is waiting for me.

But now I belong here. In the streets that aren't quite the same streets I knew before, and in the place that for want of a better name I call the palace. The glass castle is another name for it, the fairy citadel if you want to be fancy. Anyway, I can enter it from here, although if I understand the boy correctly I could enter it from anywhere if I knew what I was about. And it isn't only an edifice, as those names might suggest, but a realm. Certain images recur, familiar to me in some sense, but never exactly staying still. The yew, the hound, the signet, the cards, the crows, and so on. I don't just see them, and know them. I become them. I don't know what they mean and it becomes harder to write them down. The boy says I will soon see no need to, because there will be no difference between them and me. But I will have at least one more try.

Crab Apple, Old Crab Apple

I don't think there's anything more I can do here. I said it before, but now I am sure. Crabbe is not coming back, even though he sometimes seems very near. I will leave things just as they are. I can't bear to do anything with them. They will just have to stay here. Perhaps in due time the answer will become clear. The place is wind-tight, sea-secured, sufficiently. And of course I know I am leaving things just so, just in case. Just in case he does return. Yet I can't simply go back to my own place, resume matters as if nothing had happened, even though to be exact nothing has in fact happened. So I've decided to take the track away from the shore, over the marshes, the track we saw together that time, and walk my way back towards home, or wherever it goes. I have a strong feeling, or maybe it is only a hope, that I will be following him: so, who knows?

the brooding stars the Plenitude black rain the beasts the cards winged boy eastern horses travelling marshes

   winter damson starkly White birds fire blossom slow
signatures the couched yew the paws The bitter writing
the black sealing The Ancient Blue beasts the sea strangers
the red lichen the sunlight like honey luminescent The
shore The ravens' footstools

yew fire clouds   damson rain   giant black dog   fingers
sealing   winter strangers   couched lions   black as stars
red sky beasts   winged ink   The Blue Queen
      The lost cards the orders

Krabababaal

The House of Flame

In the early Spring of the year 1885, a young man of twenty-two strode into his father's study in a Monmouthshire rectory, and announced to the drowsy parson the news that a solemn nation could hardly bear to hear: in carefully rehearsed Apocalyptic Greek, he proclaimed—"Khartoum, the mighty city, has fallen, has fallen." Then he sank into an oak chair and added, in English, "General Gordon is dead." There was little else to tell: he had gleaned the news from the paper-sellers in the little village below.

A fervent youth, given to long lonely walks, A. Llewellyn Jones (as he signed himself) had followed the events leading up to the tragedy in the Sudan as keenly as anyone. A sense of foreboding had struck his soul early on as the story unfolded: Gordon, the ascetic visionary, the maverick whom some thought a little mad, departing with the barest of possessions, to journey across Europe and down the Nile, unescorted, with the aim of meeting alone the Mahdi, the leader of thousands of followers, and coming to terms with him. Soon, the messages from the heart of Africa confirmed his fears: Gordon had evacuated those he had gone to rescue, but now was himself besieged.

The boy had burned with impatience for the relief force to be announced that would go to the rescue of this strange, gallant gentleman: now he knew, in company with the whole country, that it had been sent too late. When he had gone to the dingy little town on some errand and heard the news, called in the high, urgent voices of its only two news-boys, he had felt fierce and sick at heart. On the return home, through deep lanes, by silver brooks and over the rise of domed hills, he had raged over it, and thought hard about how he might most meetly tell his father. It soon came to him that only the tongue of the heroes of old was apt for the task, and so he had remembered his lessons, and formed in his mind the solemn words.

After the clergyman had thanked his son for the news, and the manner of it, he had sighed, said he had looked for nothing better, and turned once more to his notes on the natural history of his parish, notes that were as disordered and fragmentary now as they had been for the ten or so years his son had known of them.

"There is a glass of milk and a scone in the parlour, my boy." He added, "Go you and refresh yourself—you look over-tired. The news has hit you bad, I see."

All that night, as he lay in his bed in the little room at the back of the rectory, looking out upon the orchard and the quaint garden, and across to the darkened woods on the hills, Llewellyn Jones felt his form was restless with fever. He had read how careless his hero was of the things of the body, the privations he accepted without a word, the voluntary poverty. His own days in the city had given him a taste of such austerity: he had lived on green tea, dry bread, and dark tobacco, his attic room as bare as any hermit's. There he had tried his vocation in literature, fierce to find the word and phrase that would make the page burn. And now his thoughts returned to the fate endured by Charles George Gordon, a great soldier, a gentleman, a prophet, and a martyr. What could he do to now honour his memory, to make his own life fit for his hero? He must return to the city, this he knew, and search for the signs of his mission.

The trees on the horizon were stark against the empurpled sky, like cloaked watchmen at the gates of a vast palace. A solitary amber light glinted in the depths of the hills: it was perhaps simply a farmer abroad with a sick beast, but it seemed to him like a lamp of vigil at some hidden shrine. Through the window came the sound of the clear cold running of the stream in the brake, and a rare breath, as of the exhalations of silver angels, seeped into his room. And the boy knew that he was a witness to all that was holy in the world, and must make himself a chalice for the pouring-out of the precious sacral wine.

The word had come not long after that there would be work for him in London, at the office of a publisher, if he would take it: and so he had said farewell once more to the country of his youth, and returned to the bare cell and the meagre food he had relished once before. By day and night, he catalogued, edited, and wrote a book out of all his curious learning in the byways of literature. He followed the news that came from Khartoum, and within him still kept the idea of performing some homage to his hero, though he could not yet see his way. All around, he heard of statues and busts put up to the lost figure, of memorial services, of subscriptions, of schools, streets and parks named for him. Yet all these, he knew, were tokens of a moment: the effigies would grow stained, the foundations become mired in administration, the signs would fade, and over the years the memory of Gordon would be reduced to a few lines. What he sought was some finer, more enduring service of the spirit.

And then there came that passing of chance that can sometimes seem like a greater tremor in the order of things, a sleight of the hand of fate.

He had reported to the untidy, threadbare, stale office of the publisher to find what work he had for him that day, and the cheerful fellow had thrown into his arms a slim pale book, with the words, "Here, this'll interest you. One thou. review by Monday." Llewellyn Jones was at first crestfallen: he had his own choice reading to hand, and very often the books sent for review in the publisher's rambling journal were of the narrowest interest. To spin out one thousand words on some trivial volume, when he might be deep in the pages of a Browne or a De Quincey, might be a minor agony. But he thought of his place, his perilous hold on this ledge of literature, and said nothing.

He turned the book over and read the lettering, in a sort of debased font of chapel-black: REFLECTIONS IN PALESTINE, followed, in lower letters, by the word GORDON. A candle-flame quickened inside him. Surely it could not be? He regarded the book more closely. Yes, there it was. Silly scrollwork had been made over the title letters of the front cover, but still stark and clear was the plain name—CHARLES GEORGE GORDON. His fingers flickered through the pages of the book and he caught glimpses of some reference to the skull hill of Golgotha, and later to the indwelling of the Holy Ghost. Dazed, for a few moments the publisher's office reeled before him, seemed to tilt on a hidden axis, and he felt as though some impulse from the book had passed through his fingers and into his body. He put the precious work carefully into the little satchel he carried, and all that day thought gladly of the words that awaited him at night in his dim room, as he read the book by candle-light, all oblivious of the city murmuring below.

After he climbed the stairs to his austere retreat, and ate his frugal repast, he lit two pale tapers with simple ceremony, took out the book with reverence, and read the opening pages. Gordon, it seemed, had spent some time in the year before his immolation, in the Holy Land. He had wanted to find the true sites of the life and passion of Christ in Jerusalem, and had mapped and plotted the old city with his surveyor's knowledge and care. The first part of the book detailed his conclusions.

But the second part departed from this task, and Gordon instead meditated upon his faith, and shared his certainties. There were things here, Llewellyn soon saw, not to be found in the overt dogmas of any organised church: the ardent words of a man who had thought deeply and alone, until he had winnowed out his own way of knowing. He seemed to have a particular devotion to the idea of the Holy Ghost, that most attenuated and least-understood Person of the Trinity. And yet, to Llewellyn, brought up as a parson's son in the knowledge of the teachings of the church, it seemed to him that Gordon's maxims trod the verges of the heterodox. They were more akin to some of the speculations of the hermetic philosophers he had studied when cataloguing occult books. "The fleshly mind is enmity," Gordon averred, and it "cannot receive the Holy Ghost". We must concern ourselves with no mortal portion, but with a rarer feast. For Union with the Holy Ghost is "exactly the eating of the tree of life": and the "indwelling of the Holy Ghost is the Alpha and Omega of all life".

The boy found these sentences mysteriously thrilling. For had not he, it is true by force of circumstance, abjured all that was fleshly, and devoted himself instead to the rarest essences of thought? Could not he be numbered among those who were readied to taste of the fruit of the tree of life? His dark eyes glimmered in the light of the tapers and he felt his olive skin tingle with a strange rapture. He got up and paced the narrow confines of his cabin high above the city. The flames of the candles flickered as his form passed to and fro in its restlessness. At last, he thought that he could not contain the zeal he felt, and he must go out into the streets, even if only to let the dark air assuage his spirit.

It was by no means the first time he had taken his perplexities out into the London night. At times, his mean room had become intolerable to him, and the words on the pages he turned, the labyrinthine passages of Urquhart, say, or Robert Burton, became like incantations before his eyes, and he would find it necessary to walk off the spell for a while in wider vistas. Therefore, he knew the ways of the city well in its guise as the realm of Napthalia, the domain of the gas lamps. He had seen the garish yellow glare feud with the shadows, noted the glittering pools of amber ebb upon the shores of the darkness. Now, as he walked, a stray freshet of air blew upon his face, and though it had an under-breath of the fetid, it still called dimly to mind the breezes that played upon the green slopes of his home country. If here he could not stray among deep hollowed lanes, or let his gaze rise to the sombre haze of the hills, he could at least let his way take him to the most obscure and secret quarters. There would be tokens and talismans of the true country: a stark planc tree forlorn in a lonely square, its upper limbs lost in a mauve mist; a drinking fountain with the face of a silenus in corroded bronze, dribbling a pale green ichor; or, in the distance, the spire of some archaic citadel, studded with blackened stone crockets, and lofting in the gloom.

Yet as he stalked along the dim and echoing streets, there ran through him like quicksilver the ideas he had read in Charles Gordon's book—that a part of the Holy Ghost is always within us, that we ourselves are a house of spirit, that only in the sanctuary lamp of our soul can the deity flourish. And he pondered upon Gordon's quest for the true shrines of Jerusalem—what was its inner meaning? If we are indeed each a semblance of the Holy Ghost walking abroad in this world, a white flame wandering in the darkened ways, then surely the holy city must be found in all places, even in the lineaments of London—the temple, the mount and the tomb must lie all about us, though hidden to profane eyes.

In the alleyways, among the streaked gutters and the offal, he caught sight of the pale crooked faces of street urchins, like goblin lanterns, and remembered how he had heard that Gordon had taken these from their mean surroundings, bathed, fed, clothed and educated them, and exalted them as his "kings", who would go out into the world annealed, anointed and armed, to spread his word of the Holy Ghost. That such gargoyles, who sneered at him now from their huddled dens, could be turned into princes seemed to him strange, almost miraculous. And yet it was so—and he wondered what then might be accomplished for him, hardly less poor, who had also heard and understood Gordon's call.

Nor were these stray children all that there was of the sordid. At times he passed blazing doorways where thick, fuddled voices called out blasphemies. Scabbed dogs ran from the kicks of their drunken masters. Women in grey, frayed gowns slunk from out of the shadows as he passed, and tried to detain him with whispered promises and entreaties, pushing the lank hair back from their temples. The faces of the last city revellers, all in their soiled finery, were worse still: they each seemed fixed in a grotesque, queasy leer, as if a mask had been seared into their flesh.

Yet all this did not taint him, for in the fever of his journeying, he seemed scarcely of this world. As he made his hurried way through the city, he felt that he hardly had any form, that his whittled body was a house of flame, a lamp of fabulous, fragile glass, holding within an ever-burning light. All the days and nights of his duress, his privation, seemed to him now keen and holy pleasures; they were as the preparations of an acolyte for a great revelation. And he remembered his mission, and gazed about him for the secret signs of Jerusalem in the black stones of the metropolis.

As the night wore on, his pace became stiffened, and it was only with slow, deliberate treads that he was able to continue. He found himself in an outer region unknown even to him in his widest wanderings. Stuccoed villas drew back from the street as if they were marbled senators raised upon plinths, lifting up their toga-like walls from the throng. The streetlamps were fewer, and the rutted roads, as if they yearned for the fields beyond, gathered up wan grasses in their channels. He knew that he must soon find a place to rest. The sullen houses were all in darkness, so that he could hardly even beg for a drink of water at the back door. There was not so much as a cabman's shelter. He began to succumb to doubt. Why had he come out here, so far from his room, which, though it was dim and narrow, held his books, and his pages of manuscript, his black tobacco and his bitter green tea? What had driven him across the dark face of the city into this dreary quarter, which flickered before his eyes as if it were made of the shadows from a guttering candle?

And then he summoned into his mind the curious words of Charles Gordon, in the book that had been made of his letters from Palestine. He thought of the General's last days in the Governor's Palace at Khartoum, still studying scripture, still steadfast in his acceptance of his fate. He had gone out to meet his foes, they said, with a fierce solemnity. He had written that the Holy Ghost was upon him, and he knew that all would be as it must.

What did this mean for him, A. Llewellyn Jones, a worker in the backwaters of literature, unknown, unseen by the myriads of the city? He was not destined for the military, that he knew: he doubted, indeed, with a sudden lunge of understanding, if that had even been Gordon's true vocation. Those who devoted themselves to this strange prophet's memory were also, ultimately, on the wrong track. It was not as curators of the achievements of others that we lived. Steadily, he began to see his way: it was in the proclamation of Jerusalem in the city, of Tsion in the country; he must write with all his art, all his curious learning, all his understanding, of—what was Gordon's word?—of the indwelling. And he felt steal over him an exaltation and a terror: he knew, even in his weariness, that his way would be met by many with scorn, and that the riches of the earth would not be his.

His route had taken him far to the East, and on the horizon he thought he saw the first lifting of the veils of night, and a blue glimmering beyond, like the clear gaze of pale eyes. To one side of the track where he now stood, he saw a wicket gate of wrought iron in a boundary wall. A grove of yew trees formed an arched corridor leading from the entrance. He took slow steps towards this, his feet sore and bruised. The handle yielded to his touch, and he passed through the gate, and trod softly below the evergreen penumbra. He caught the ancient scent of the yew trees upon his breath, and it seemed to spiral through his limbs. There was a stone gazebo beyond, hollowed in the further wall. A scrolled bench was already glistening with the dew of the morning. He sank down upon it, and felt the chill quicken him. The crowns of bright wild flowers swayed upon their stalks. He watched them steadily. For he did not know whether he had entered now a new Eden, or Gethsemane.

The Seventh Card

Mr. Warringer disapproved of receiving Christmas cards at the beginning of December or even, what was worse, in late November: as indeed he found himself obliged to disapprove of quite a few other things these days. His own habit was to send his cards at the last possible occasion in order for them to arrive just before the festive day. The season of Christmas, as he was wont to tell such of his acquaintances who found themselves under the necessity of listening, begins, not ends, on December 25th, and greetings must therefore mark that commencement, and not some lengthy, indeterminate and inappropriate prior period. He was also inclined to reminisce about the days when one could post a card on the morning of Christmas Eve and be sure it would be delivered in the evening post of the same day. He had, in fact, never known such a service himself, but he had heard tell of it in books, and people seemed willing to believe he really was as old as all that.

There was, it must be admitted, an added advantage of sending one's cards so late, which was that it meant you need only issue one to those who had sent one to you. There was thus no question of venturing a card that would not be reciprocated. To this end, one or two days before the last date intimated by the post office, he assembled such cards as he had received onto the narrow strip of the gatefold table left by leaving down the unused parts, and then began to mark up his list. This was made the easier because Mr. Warringer already maintained a schedule of his friends and acquaintances. The two categories were kept separate. Occasionally an individual was moved up from "acquaintance" to "friend" or even, dread demotion, down to the lower category. As well as the column of names, there was also, across from each, a horizontal series of rectangles, which were marked at the top of the page "M", "L", "C", "T", and "O". These stood for "Meeting", "Letter", "Card", "Telephone", and "Other". It was Mr. Warringer's habit to enter in pencil in the long narrow boxes the most recent date on which one or the other of these forms of contact had transpired. The Other box was not often used as he was not quite sure what it might be for, but he was a prudent man and thought it might be useful for some as yet uncertain eventuality.

It being the evening of the 20th, when he got home from work, Mr. Warringer judged it the correct time to write his cards, address the envelopes, affix second-class stamps, and have them ready to take to the post. But before beginning to write his cards, Mr. Warringer shuffled those he had received into their several different types, as it was a mild amusement of his to see what was the fashion in designs that year. The categories were of his own devising. Flora and Fauna generally comprised robins, reindeer, holly, mistletoe, and so on. "Ye Olde", as he termed it, involved stagecoaches, or carol singers in Victorian garb. Weather encompassed all snowy scenes not involving birds, beasts, or historic figures. Ornaments meant Christmas trees, baubles, glittery snowflakes, etc. "Pious" depicted nativity scenes, whether of the manger, the shepherds, or the wise men. In some years, he also reluctantly had to admit a "Miscellaneous" category but on the whole he deprecated this and tried always to fit such irregular examples into one of his main and immemorial classifications. He was dismayed to see that this year "Ornaments" easily outstripped "Pious", and "Ye Olde" was once again ascending. However, there were at least no cards that he could not in all conscience slot into one of his preferred terms.

Taking each of the small piles in order, he began to mark in the "C" column the date of receipt of each card, which he had written in pencil on the back of the cards on the day they arrived. At the end of this proceeding, he found himself with a card whose sender he did not know. And this, he reflected rather bitterly, had been the case in a succession of years before. He had put the card in the "Weather" category because it depicted a landscape of, not snow, but frost. At least, he supposed that must be what was intended. It was a completely barren scene in monochrome. A black road led in a long curve towards some dim pale hills, and on the black road was a sort of scintillant quality, achieved by the artist, so he supposed, by some form of stippling. Dark wayside trees held up their haggard limbs rather too like imploring hands. There was no sign of any comforting lantern, no trundle of the mailcoach, no cottage with glowing windows, no perky redbreast, no loping questing hare, not a thing indeed except the wintry aspect to exemplify the season. And it seemed to Mr. Warringer that each year he received a card with a very similar aspect to this one, though not quite the same, and each year he was unable to identify the sender. There was no message inside and the signature, a scribble in black ink, was indecipherable. It resembled the bleak bare hedgerow of the picture, a matter of thorns and woody claws.

Each year, and this he calculated was the seventh, Mr. Warringer speculated anew as to which of his acquaintances (it could scarcely be a friend) might be responsible. In some previous years he had scrutinised the envelope to see whether the postmark might afford some clue as to the sender, but he had found that invariably this was smudged and indistinct, as indeed was the handwriting inside. One theory he had entertained was that the card must be that of some tradesman, the hurried script suggesting one who has many such to write and finds it rather a chore. Such a personage would also not be daunted by receiving no reciprocating card, since he was after all in a supplicatory position and must not necessarily expect the condescension of his customers or clients. But on the other hand it was, as Mr. Warringer all too often observed, the habit of tradesmen to imprint the name and mark of their business prominently upon their cards, thus turning them into a form of cheap advertisement: and there was no such publicity here. So a tradesman the sender probably was not.

Furthermore, Mr. Warringer saw that of his list of correspondents only two had not sent a card, and in both cases he had scarcely expected one. Tubby Whiting, a distant college friend, was one of those vague individuals to whom the calendar and indeed the diary was a closed mystery, and whose letters, when they arrived, were often dated with the preceding year. Further, his manuscript was large and billowy, rather like his person, and not at all like the stark hand on the card. Whereas Bristle, who had once been a neighbour and fellow chess club member, was a confirmed atheist who never sent cards on principle. If he were to do so, reflected Mr. Warringer, they might well be just such cards as this one, bleak and devoid of reference to religion, and further he suspected Bristle of possessing a crabbed hand like this dark dash of shadow inside, but his acquaintance's vehement opposition to the whole business put the matter beyond such conjecture. There was thus really no void in his chart of associates which might be filled by this irksome card.

He picked it up once more and stared both at the austere landscape and at the dark signature. There began to form a suspicion.

The next day Mr. Warringer took the train as usual through the numerous stations to his place of employment, nodding briefly to the few fellow regular passengers he found it unavoidable thus to recognise. He worked in the cathedral city for the Chaplain's Library, an obscure relic of old publishing law. Once printing had begun to flourish, and the authorities became distinctly wary of it, they naturally introduced both a monopoly, which was held by the Stationers' Company, and a censorship, which was maintained by the Church. Thus, all publications relating to Divinity, which was interpreted very broadly and included prophecy, astrology and alchemy, had then to be approved by the Chaplain to the Archbishop. Copies of all such items had to be lodged with the Chaplain's Library for prior approval. Oddly, this meant the Church found itself licensing almanacs and prognostications, which were enormously popular and could not very well be suppressed. Which is why, in between the horoscopes and omens and phases of the moon and agricultural intelligence, these pamphlets usually took care to include a few pious interjections.

The law requiring books on Divinity and related subjects to be sent to the Chaplain's Library had never been repealed, though it had been modified by a more tolerant age so that the censorship element was removed. Its offices, in keeping with its reduced role, had been moved in the late nineteenth century to the care of one of the minor dioceses. The obligation to supply copies was now justified on the grounds of preserving an ancient custom (an argument always carrying a certain weight with an essentially sentimental nation) and, with perhaps more rational force, by the idea of maintaining an authoritative reference collection. It must also be admitted that the insistence upon the regulation was far from strict, and the Library simply accepted whatever it was sent by the routine of the more conscientious or incurious of publishers.

Mr. Warringer had when a student taken a summer job at the library as a cataloguer, but had then, as he often remarked, "stayed on a bit". Some twenty-seven years, indeed. It was methodical work and though the pay was lowly he liked the history of it all, and its largely unvarying nature suited him. Some of the stuff that came in, he admitted, *was* quite interesting. There were all sorts of tracts, treatises, and "improving" works. The two established members of staff who were there then, Mr. Urick and Miss Dearsley, would have their own fun with the student summer cataloguers, though it was all very amiable. They would quietly hand them to catalogue some of the effusions of a particularly prolific author who issued his own publications, oh! so many of them, from what was presumably his home and printed on what appeared to be a very old and temperamental duplicating machine.

Mr. Warringer had operated one of these devices himself, as it happened, for a model railway society to which he had then belonged. It was used for their newsletter. He typed the contents up on long thin skeins, like peeled flesh, and wrapped these round a revolving cylinder that was full of ink. With luck it transposed the stuff onto some absorbent sheets of paper. To his dismay, there was a tendency for the ink to get everywhere, with a particular attraction to his cuffs.

The publications from this author were not easy to catalogue because the title was not always obvious from among an eruption of phrases on the cover or title page, and furthermore he was always changing his name, his house's name, and the name of his imprint. Also, sometimes his primitive printing machine evidently got decidedly petulant and all the text and the numbers (there were quite a lot of those too) were either grey and ethereal like flakes of ash, or dashed across the page in black gouts.

As his current colleagues indulged his little joke that he was still only a "temporary", he retained responsibility for this prolific individual's output. And he still dutifully worked through them, and, to the surprise of these colleagues, actually seemed to like working out all about them, as they came in. There was at least one a week, often several. Of course, he was not required to actually read the items received except as was needed to get the details for the catalogue, but sometimes Mr. Warringer did idly flick through them, and even began to find them interesting, in a way. They were mostly speculations upon, and elaborations of, scriptural prophecy, sometimes with highly original interpretations. Occasionally he would suddenly emerge from browsing in these pages to find that quite some minutes had passed and he had been all-too-absorbed by the curious tracts. Mr. Warringer wondered if there was in fact a dynasty or lineage of these authors, one handing on to another, as was the case with the almanacs he handled, Old Merlin and Salamander stretching back several centuries.

Mr. Warringer walked the ten minutes from the station in a thoughtful mood. The library was in a corner of the Close, in an eighteenth century building of quiet elegance which he found soothing. There was a constant smell of wood polish and baked dust. He went up the tiled stairs and entered through the oak door into his own small office. He gazed briefly out of the window through the good glass onto the green below, which was still crisp from the wintry morning air. The book trolley had already been parked not far from his desk, containing recently received volumes. He took up a stack of fawn index cards and arranged them neatly before him, and then reached out for the first on the pile. But instead of picking it up and beginning the day's work, he sank back in his chair and began once more to ponder.

The suspicion that had formed the evening before returned to his thoughts. He sifted through the books on the trolley and found, as he expected, the latest utterance from the prolific author. It was, as almost always, a sheaf of foolscap stapled together and the primitive drawing on the front was the usual scattering of smudged lines. He turned to the title page. The author was presently calling himself "Brother Israfel", his house "The End House", and his press "Omega". The address of The End House was rather incongruously completed by the street name of Moor Road, followed by Curtinghall, Northamptonshire.

The library clerk found he could not say what exactly it was about the publication, and all those that had come before, which caused him to associate it with the provoking card. If he tried to form a definite explanation, it did not quite cohere. But there was something in the style of the stark artwork, and some exclamatory quality to the signature, which made him connect the two. The more he stared at the publication and turned its pages to and fro, the stronger the idea grew upon him. It was almost as if the grey monograph itself was whispering to him, fostering his suspicions. He shook his head in an effort to disperse this influence, yet found he was soon drawn back to thinking about the cold, hollow scene on the card, the stark barbed signature, and this implacable treatise.

Quite how the publisher could have got hold of his domestic and not office address he could not fathom. The only thing he could suppose was that once, in writing out the receipt to send, he had in a moment of inattention (which would be unlike him) put down his own address, though this would be quite unnecessary since the pre-printed acknowledgements already had at their head that of the Chaplain's Library. Still, it was possible. The other explanation, that Brother Israfel (or any of his previous manifestations) had noted his name so frequently seen on the receipts and looked him up in some directory or even telephoned the office to find out about him, was even less acceptable than the idea that he had made a slip.

It was not a matter he wished to encourage and he decided to adjust things to a different footing. Having carefully written out the acknowledgement and addressed the envelope, he added to this one of the official pictorial note-cards occasionally used for significant correspondents. It was graced by a drawing of the library and some of the adjoining buildings in the Close and might just pass for a card of the "Ye Olde" variety. He added a brisk "Compliments of the Season", a sufficiently neutral phrase, signed it with a flourish, added it to the envelope, and put it in his out tray. If he were wrong about his unknown Christmas correspondent, no harm was done in sending a card from the library to such a regular contact anyway: and if he were right, he was making it tactfully plain that such communications should be sent to the office and not to his home. Either way, his gesture, he felt, was seemly and correct. He began work upon the other books on the trolley.

The card could not, however, have been quite banished from his mind because, some two days later, on the night of the 23rd, he found himself dreaming about it. Or rather about the activities of its putative sender. He was in some sort of a cellar where a number of vast machines were issuing reams of smeared paper from their rolling and never-stopping drums. The grey pages cascaded at a great pace, rising up into the air and floating all around like a great flock of dingy birds, and then descending to form untidy, unsteady ziggurats. He tried putting these into proper neat columns, tried clutching at those soaring in the air, but his efforts were defeated by the constant onrush of new pages. And his anxious chasing around was not assisted by the figures of Tubby Whiting, who kept asking what day it was ("Too late! Too late!" he replied), and the sardonic Bristle, who enjoyed telling him this was what came of sending Christmas cards, especially to strangers. At the same time leering figures in overalls, aprons or suits presented him with accounts marked "Final" together with cards stamped with their own garish and vulgar emblems.

The rumbling of the machines was still in his hearing when he woke up to the cold morning of Christmas Eve. His customary three cups of tea and two slices of toast, cut diagonally into exact triangles, did not restore his equanimity. He sat over the brown dregs and the damp crumbs feeling disconsolate. The office was closed today and the truth was he had nowhere particular to go and nothing particular to do. He had already concluded all of the business of Christmas with his customary efficiency. The idea that then came to him was one he knew he must resist, but it would persist. He tried to busy himself with other things. He checked that his correspondence chart was quite up to date. He took down all the cards he had received and put them into their categories again, then shuffled them and replaced them at random on the mantelpiece and the dresser and the bookshelves. And at last, when it was still only mid-morning, he succumbed. He consulted a gazetteer and a timetable, packed a small valise, put on his hat and coat, took a last look around to make sure everything was quite in order, closed the door, and headed for the station.

It took him several changes and some time spent in waiting rooms, in each of which he had plenty of opportunity for reflection, and to reproach himself for this foolhardy journey, but not quite to the extent of reversing it. He had, after all, paid for his ticket. The people about him seemed busy and harassed, some laden with parcels or shopping, many red-faced, but all of them, in a rather desperate and joyless way, fiercely busy. He felt set apart from them, since his own activity was conducted according to the slow jolting pace of the little branch lines on which he must travel, and these frequent waiting interludes in between them. At last, however, at the dwindling of the day, he came to the final halt on his journey. It possessed a single draughty building and a single solemn porter. He asked for directions. The fellow masticated the ends of his moustache for a quite measurable period and then gave hesitant and doubtful advice. Mr. Warringer set off from the lonely platform.

It was, as the porter had warned him, a long walk. The thin pale clouds seemed stretched taut across the sky and were already being overwritten by the dim grey of dusk. The road stretched on before him like a great streak of dried ink, curving and darting as if it were a hurried signature. The trees on either side raised gnarled fingers. In the distance the hills were faded smudges. Letting his thoughts wander as he trudged on, he remembered that he had not been quite right about Christmas beginning on the 25th, for now he called to mind that in the olden times, the very ancient times, festivals always ran from nightfall, not from daybreak, so that Christmas proper, in the true tradition, began at Christmas Eve. Therefore it must be beginning now. But there was nothing here to denote it. No snow, certainly, though a harsh clarity in the air which must be a harbinger of a frost. No robin, no scurrying woodland creature, no carol singers, indeed no light whatever across the fields or in the hills.

He certainly must be upon the Moor Road, for all around was a lonely waste. But the village or settlement or whatever it was that was called Curtinghall was nowhere to be seen. Perhaps it was no more than the designation of some vague and theoretical district, made upon the map to make things tidy and complete. And as for The End House, he now had no idea where that might be. The porter had not exactly heard of it either, but had sketched out where he supposed it ought to be. But there was certainly no sort of ending in sight and for that matter no particular beginning. Mr. Warringer caught himself listening for the rumbling of the primitive printing machine, for he did not suppose it would be idle even on such a day, such an eve, as this. But nothing disturbed the silence. Another thought struck him, and he looked out for the reassuring scarlet of a pillar box (and a staunch one it must be to receive all the post issued from Omega). But there was no such flash of colour in all the drab terrain. There might, he supposed, at some point be a light when the moor gave out, and there might be stars if the clouds ever cleared, but neither of these had been shown to him yet.

The night, the Christmas night, was now descending upon him in all its brittle blackness. And by now he was becoming quite certain, and suspected even more that his hunch about the sender of the cards was correct. He knew that he had earlier been traversing the scene on the seventh card, and might indeed still be within it. And then a further thought struck him, so that he tried to remember what exactly had been on the other six. They were all much alike, and yet there were minor differences. Perhaps the way was narrower, the hills closer in, the trees more wind-torn. He wondered what other differences there might be and whether he would notice, or if the changes would be imperceptible. He also thought about how long it would take to walk through them all, one after the other, and then what he should find at the end. The first card was so long ago that he could not really recall it in the least.

It would take all night to walk them all, that was certain, and he was already weary, but the air was keen and fresh and he could, he supposed, stop and rest when he wanted, leaning perhaps against the elder trees. If he were to list his acquaintances now, he thought, they would be "Road", "Tree", "Cloud", "Frost", "Moor". Indeed, they were more than acquaintances, more even than friends. The black track seemed to be caused by his own gaze, the wracked trees were like his own limbs. The clouds and the moors might be simply the forms of his thoughts, and the frost was his own quickening. And it occurred to him as he walked on that perhaps now he had after all found a use for the column called "Other".

And maybe the parakeet was correct

I found Cyril feeding pensively his parakeet, which was perched on a dented and rather streaked globe, with cubes of melon. After the bird condescended to accept each titbit, the rotund editor wiped the juice from his fingers onto the chalk-striped cloth covering his broad thighs.

When the bird declined any further melon, Cyril emptied sunflower seeds into the palm of his hand from an ancient funerary urn and offered these instead. The parakeet scooped some into its beak, but scattered most of them onto the floor. I was far from sure that either the fruit or the seeds were what the bird ought to eat, but as Cyril himself liked them, he seemed to assume the bird must too.

He had once published four of my poems and on another occasion a vignette about cricket played in a wintry twilight. Now I had another idea and I wanted him to sponsor it. I put the idea to him. He listened in a sort of abstracted way. When I came to the crucial point, I saw him recoil.

"Football?" he murmured, "Oh, I don't know, you know, I mean really . . . "

"The game of the people," I reminded him. Cyril liked to think he had proletarian sympathies, to the extent that these didn't interfere with his own largely sybaritic pursuits.

"Yes, yes, I suppose so," he agreed.

"In any case, European football," I said, pressing home my case. "Who writes about that? No-one knows very much about it."

"My dear fellow," he demurred, with a shudder, "I don't even know much about the English, um, houses or sides, or whatever it is they call them."

"Besides," I went on, "I would really be writing about the people, the culture, the land. Football would just be a—well, a symbol, a motif."

"I see," he replied, still doubtfully, "and would you really rather do this than offer me some more of your delightful, if admittedly minor, poetry?"

"I expect I might do both."

There was a bit more hovering around of this kind before, with a deep sigh, Cyril at last conceded he would cough up for four essays loosely linked to football on the Continent, provided they were more like travel writing than sports reporting. The parakeet looked at me with its habitual sideways tilt of the head as I departed, as if it too entertained doubts as to the wisdom of my idea.

The idea had come to me in a rain-ridden January when I was sitting on a folding chair in the press box at Windsleigh Town's ground. The press box was in fact a small tent with its flaps open to the pitch. It was called a marquee, of course, but I suspected it came from army surplus. The rain drove maliciously across the field into where we sat, the game was scrappy, the few hundred spectators muted and bedraggled. Not for the first time, I wondered what I was doing here in such dreary surroundings. The answer, of course, was that poetry and picturesque prose didn't pay, whereas reporting on provincial soccer did, even if sparingly.

It wasn't that difficult either. I only had to produce four or five paragraphs at most. Bill Tench, who was usually sent to the same games as me by our main rival, had it all worked out. Over the years he'd developed an argosy of suitable phrases, and simply jumbled together whichever of them seemed to fit, without too much attention to what actually happened on the pitch. Most of the time he was either dozing or boozing.

As I looked across at him with his head lolling against the soiled collar of a raincoat that might once have been fawn-coloured, I knew I had to get away, or else there was every chance I might end up like him. Besides, I wanted to be free of this sodden grey island and go somewhere strange and exotic. How could I work it? One of my few advantages was a pretty good gift for tongues, which the interception corps had brushed up further for me in the war.

Eventually even my rusted cogs clunked into position. They played football over there, didn't they? Had some different styles too, I'd heard. I'd seen the Hungarians in an exhibition match once, a welcome relief from the boot and trudge of the lower divisions here—fluent, stylish, intelligent. Yet none of our great daily papers ever had much of a word about the overseas game. Could I get myself a sort of roving commission to cover the big teams, the big matches, over there?

No, I couldn't. They wouldn't bite. Readers not interested, they said. Not the real stuff, you know. All about local pride, you see. A paragraph on Grimthorpe Athletic's grinding goalless draw with the Mechanical Engineers was worth more than one on Royal Madrid, or Athletic Club Ravenna, or Paris-Vite. So Cyril was pretty much my last chance. Of course, getting him to agree was different to getting him to publish, which was different again to getting him to pay. But it was a start. So I packed a narrow bag and booked a boat passage. I hoped that once he saw the sort of thing I had in mind, he might extend the somewhat grudgingly-agreed four essays into six, and then beyond.

I proceeded cautiously. The first piece was a stroke of luck. Knowing of Cyril's affection for odd birds, I filed a piece about an old gent in Dieppe, a Spanish exile whom I got talking to in a café.

"Once, in the stadium in the city," he told me, "I saw the one they called 'The Stork'. He was tall, long-legged, thin, you see? That day he scored a goal you could never forget. I have never forgotten it. He was like a ghost. Dressed all in white, of course, their kit, you understand? He suddenly appeared!"

He made a movement with his hand like a paper plane floating down.

"From the left, naturally, that was where he always played. But he was an apparition that day. An apparition! Also, it was as if the defenders had been turned to stone. They were like statues. Can you imagine . . . " here he took a sip from the brandy I'd provided, and his eyes gleamed, "a phantom in an old garden? A palace garden. Something floats past the statues. That was him, that was The Stork that day. Do you know what was strange? After the goal, there was silence. Not a roar, not a cheer. At least, not at first. In all that big stadium, everything was quiet. Then of course we all gave tongue, yes, we did."

"Well," he continued, "I was telling them one day in the village about this, and you know I might have told them it before, so they just carried on at the draughts board, or reading a newspaper, or simply watching the passers-by in the square, just as we used to do . . . " Here he paused, and looked away from me for a moment, then sighed and screwed up his leathery face and said, "And what do you think? Over there,"—he gestured, pointing upwards, as if he were indeed still in his village among his *compadres*, "just as I was finishing my story, as I have told it to you, a great white stork landed on the old nest on top of the bell-tower. He floated in from nowhere. We had seen no stork there for many years. But today—that day, you see? The Stork arrives. I said to them, watch out! Watch what he does, that one. Some day he will kick the sun or moon out of the sky! Yes, from his nest, he will draw back his leg and then—whoosh!" And he got up from his chair and made an energetic movement to illustrate this.

Well, that was picturesque enough. I added a few facts about the career of The Stork, the team in the capital that he played for, and their rivals, and the league they played in, and how they differed from English teams. I reminded readers that so far neither the sun nor the moon had been seen sailing towards any celestial net, but said that The Stork was always stealthy and who could say what might happen one day, and then I sent it off. A few weeks later I got a postcard from Cyril in his dark-inked, rounded hand, like a row of slightly squashed blackberries, to say he supposed it would do.

The second report I sent him was about an obscure football field with a goal-post that was situated pretty much exactly on the border between two countries. You could take a shot in Luxembourg and score a goal in Belgium, or so it was said. I didn't even bother going to look at that one because it sounded a bit too neat to be true, and was probably some sort of local joke. I picked up the story in a bar in Rotterdam, along with a lot of other less printable yarns. The Dutch were one of the first to pick up the idea of football and had some good teams still. So I added some discussion of soccer in the Low Countries, carefully explained to me by the conscientious drinkers of Rotterdam, to plump it out a bit. However, the piece also afforded the opportunity for some pious remarks on the absurdity of borders, which I thought would accord with Cyril's internationalist outlook, as he liked to think, and this piece, too, got a brief acceptance.

After this I went to Italy, which also had a very thriving league, and wrote what I liked to think of as a delicate vignette about a team that played on a pitch in the South situated among ancient Greek ruins, trying to weave in some suggestion that they were the heirs to the Corinthian and Spartan athletic traditions—because I knew Cyril was a fervent Philhellene, as well as having a fondness for lithe and tawny young men, whom I tried to evoke alluringly. Anyway, it worked, and I got a note reminding me "just one more please".

For the last story, I decided to write about street football in Paris. Why not? I wanted to go there anyway and I knew some of the run-down quarters where the Apaches played. I was going to say, because I knew what my story line would be before I got there, that this was where the soul of football was, where there were ragged coats for goalposts, soot-streaked walls for grandstands, and a ball that was hard and half-deflated, and looked like a giant walnut. Also, I wanted to get a sense of the mystery of the back streets in there, because I knew Cyril liked a hint of the singular. "I have a melancholy, my child," he once said to me, "a *cafard* of the soul, which only the promise of the strange will assuage." Well, he got that, all right.

It was late when I left the café in the rue-de-Bonnes-Enfants and headed for the congeries of alleyways leading north from there, narrow passages where the *enfants*, shall we say, not-quite-so-good, might be found, the sort that kick a ball around in the street and greet strangers with insolence and derision. For which I rather liked them. There was a dark greasy sheen on the cobblestones which the dim lanterns hardly diminished, those that had not been broken. After wandering further and further in, I at last heard not too far away the brittle, fragmented cries of boys' voices and the sort of scuttle and thud that suggested a scratched-together game. I could not at first quite discern the source of these sounds. But after several more turnings between high walls, I glimpsed, at the end of one to my left, the grey figures flickering in the dim light.

I slowed my pace and approached cautiously. The black brick corridor was strewn with the slats of broken crates, yellow newspapers, crushed cigarette packets. I could make out six or seven urchins pounding about at the end of the alley. One set of coat goal-posts were there all right, and the ball, from what I could see, was indeed gnarled and misshapen. There was a fierce, a passionate determination on the faces of the players. Kicks were aimed as much at legs as at the ball, tackles and charges were simply a thrusting rush, with no thought for finesse. Hair and ears were tugged, and there was a lot of loud, exaggerated spitting.

As I watched from a careful distance, leaning into the wall, I began to work out that there were not two sides in this game, but every boy was playing for himself. This was a hexagonal battlefield. They each wanted to get the ball and fire it at the goal, and the score was for themselves. The goalkeeper, meanwhile, the tallest of them, was against them all and did not hesitate to upend them and shove the others away in defence of the sacred space at the end of the street. Yet beneath all the arrogance and aggression I could also sense, or perhaps I merely hoped to see this, a *camaraderie*, a strong affinity between them. If one of them fell too hard and did not at first get up, the others would, once the play came to a natural stop, go over and help him up, admittedly with jeers.

I was beginning to think I had enough to write a "report" of the match, but found that I still wanted to watch. I needed a cigarette too, but thought that if I struck a light it might give me away. So I held on and continued to consider the kind of football they were playing, which was really quite removed from the organised game; it was more like some primeval ritual. Then I began to pay more attention to the calls between the players. They were not in French. That was not a particular surprise: there were many in this quarter from other places. But I could not make out what it was they spoke. I thought I knew a bit about quite a few tongues—that was one of my "qualifications" for writing about football in Europe, as I had told Cyril. This one I did not recognise, and the shouts and curses and jeers were in a curt, strange language that seemed to use a lot of "X" and "Z" or long "S" sounds. Basque? I wondered. Yet I had heard Basque when I was in Spain, and this didn't seem the same, though it might be a distant cousin. I fumbled in my pocket for a scrap of paper, found the café reckoning, and intended to try to capture the sound of their hoarse, jagged cries. But I never did get a single phrase.

Because by bad luck a wild kick sent the ball towards me and as they gazed after it and were about to give chase they saw me and stopped, and a silence fell. I pretended at once that I was just lighting my Gitanes. I drew in deeply. The smoke drifted slowly around me. Still they did not move. So I advanced the few paces towards where the ball had come to a halt against an outcrop of coltsfoot that had somehow gained a hold in the gutter. Its yellow chimney-brush head gave a burst of light. Measuring the distance, I was about to boot the ball back to them and turn away when I hesitated. It was, as I had expected, a squat misshapen thing, more leather than air. Any trade markings it once had were long scuffed away. But in the shadows here it looked as if it had a face. I bent and picked it up. I thought at first these might be chance markings, gashes from the street grit that suggested grim eyes and a leering mouth. Then I was not so sure: these were daubed marks. And as well as the lineaments of a stark face there were characters that might be letters, though not of an alphabet I knew.

Kids, I know, will draw faces anywhere. On walls, on paving stones, on their books, if they have any, on balloons, even on each other's backs in chalk or charcoal. I wonder sometimes if it's about peopling their world with their creations: "Yes, there's all of you; but I have these. These are my signs, my people." Yet I had never in fact seen a face on a football before, though I could imagine some idle youth doing it. So it wasn't so much the fact of the face, as the sort of face it was. What had been put on the ball was not the artless diagram of eyes, nose, mouth, ears that children habitually draw. It was more like the kind of face, with its raddled skin and dank grin, that you might in fact meet, if you were unlucky. And I stared at in a sort of fascination. The cluster of black signs around it only seemed to draw me in further. I thought that if I looked at them hard enough they might betray a meaning.

I walked towards them and held out the head, the ball, to the tallest figure, the goalkeeper. He made a grab, but I pulled it back.

"*Quel est le visage?*" I asked.

He shook his head, sullenly.

"*Les lettres?*" No reply.

The gang around him were restless. Their own faces were almost as hard and bleak as the ball. I found myself thinking that when they were older they might easily become what it portrayed. And then they began to murmur among themselves the syllables I had heard earlier, as if the sigils on the gnarled sphere were being released into the air.

I gestured to show that I would like to keep the ball, and I drew out my spare box of cigarettes and held it out to them. I could see the longing in their narrow dark eyes as they exchanged glances. But they would not accept. Cautiously, inside my pocket, I drew out a few notes and fluttered these in front of them. They seemed, surprisingly, of even less interest. Then I let my dignity get the better of me. Though I wanted to, I would not run down the street with their toy, their idol, with them in bawling pursuit. I saw that it would not do. So I shrugged and handed the ball back to them.

The long youth took it from me more cautiously this time and as he did so he turned the face towards him and stared at it and then at me, as if he were willing the face to transfer itself to me. Well, I don't know. It seemed that way. But maybe my imagination was a bit keyed-up by then. I offered him a cigarette again anyway but he still refused. They all stood there, waiting, petulant looks on their fierce faces, and murmuring indecipherably. I saw that they would not resume their game until I went away, and so I turned and strode briskly back along the alley. I did not look back. It took me a long time to find my way to the lighter quarters and all that time I thought I could hear their distant shouts in that curious tongue: and most of the time I was in those dark and lonely alleys I also thought I could hear footfalls not far behind me.

Laughter Ever After

Cogenhoe always associated double decker buses with town streets, so it seemed odd to him to be on one travelling through the narrow lanes of an empty countryside, especially as the number of passengers it carried from village to village never seemed to amount to more than about a dozen or thirteen. Yet though it was incongruous, it also seemed curiously comforting. He enjoyed the slow, chugging pace. And what might have been dull and monotonous was enlivened a little by a brisk breeze. The bus swayed and creaked in the wind as though it were a sailing ship. Why it was that the Combined Counties service had selected this great green galleon from its fleet for the journey he could not say. It must mean at least, he reflected, that there could not be any low bridges on the route.

He stared out of the smeared window from his top deck seat. The grey haze from his cigarette seemed to sympathise with the scudding grey cloud outside. Through this drifting, the flat fields that passed beneath his gaze were a sodden dim green. The trees, he noticed, had relinquished their dry leaves early, as if resigned already to winter. No-one, he supposed, ever came to this part of the world for pleasure, unless it was pleasure of a peculiarly perverse kind. It might be said, he decided, that pleasure was what drew him here, but it felt more of a necessity, as it often is for the fierce collector.

The bus stopped at what looked like a disused toll house, octagonal and with a conical roof and pointed-arch windows. It had once been painted mustard yellow but now the condiment had congealed. The driver turned off the engine and waited, presumably to stick to his timetable. Nobody got off and nobody got on. The sudden silence that descended was brittle. It was soon filled. A passenger further back stirred and coughed, as if he did not like the silence. Outside, leaves crept furtively along the road and jackdaws cackled. There was a weather vane on top of the toll house and Cogenhoe had a good view of it from his lofty vantage point. The restless black arrow was veering about from north to east. Scatterings of hail rattled on the bus windows. After a few minutes the engine started up again with a hoarse lurch, like a burst of laughter.

Nobody could call the town, when at last they got there, notable, but it was, Cogenhoe decided, tidy. They had pulled up in the market square. The driver stared indifferently before him as they all got off. This was where the journey ended, though not for him: he would be taking the bus back. The square, which wasn't square, had a war memorial, and black and white bollards like a row of Art Deco salt and pepper pots. Cogenhoe could see a pale town hall that looked like an attempt at a Roman temple, and a chapel in red brick Gothic. There were a lot of benches, as if people mostly spent time here waiting. A newspaper stand promised the results from the local Cribbage League.

Things seemed neat here, squared off, like a draughtsman's drawing. And now Cogenhoe felt doubtful. His real reason for coming, he began to realise, would be an intrusion into such a place of quiet, subdued civility. He hesitated, and himself took a seat on one of the benches. There was a smell of diesel oil from the bus and into this there emanated the fumes from a fish and chip shop. He gave the matter some thought and decided to offer, if asked, a version that would be more acceptable.

He went over this again as he sat in his hotel room with its mauve candlewick bedspread and its monochrome prints of scenes from *Pilgrim's Progress*. The fact was that he had come here in search of a pamphlet. Nobody else had a copy, not even the British Museum, nor the great collectors and finders: not Dolby, the eminent editor; not the great collector Latcher; nor the ingenious bookdealer Oggeling. It was, of course, the sort of thing that would be hard to find. Pamphlets hide on the shelves, caught tight between the books, or they lurk in boxes of ephemera, with guides to ancient monuments, theatre programmes, old street maps, official brochures for long-forgotten regeneration projects. This one, anyway, had never yet turned up. It was known about only by rumour, a passing reference in a study, with an evasive footnote, and a doubtful entry in some guide issued by an obscure publisher up in the wilds of Yorkshire. To tell the people here that he had come all this way in quest of a pamphlet would be to invite incredulity, he felt sure, especially as what it was said to contain was a ghost story.

Cogenhoe was an assiduous collector of ghost stories. Not, he would always patiently explain, the anecdotal, supposedly true sort: no, the literary. It was an art not disdained by the distinguished: Kipling, Buchan, Greene, Spark, among many others. And the pamphlet was supposed to be of that kind, a work of fiction. But he thought that if he were to explain this, it would make him even more culpable in the no doubt polite but nevertheless perturbed judgement of the good burghers here. And for another thing he did not want the townsfolk to know that the little publication, said to have been issued by some local society, had any great value: he must not arouse suspicion. Perhaps he might even secure a cache of them in some long-forgotten stock room, and then be able to sell them off carefully, gradually to his rivals.

Fortunately, there was a better reason for his presence, one which had the advantage of being linked to his real reason and therefore half-true. And this aspect at least was plausible, since it concerned the town's most famous son, and would be sure to appeal to civic pride. Cogenhoe remembered hearing him on the wireless in childhood, rather too often, indeed. He had found out about his local connection when he had been looking into the history of the town to inform his visit.

This was Charles Penrose, a music hall entertainer and comic turn who had had an enormous success with "The Laughing Policeman", the entire point of which was summed up by its title. It was certainly jolly, in a sort of forced way, and Cogenhoe kept an affection for it, despite its ubiquity. He had felt mildly shocked, though, by a line which urged the listener, when he encountered that eponymous official, to "shake him by his fat old hand" and "give him half a crown". Policemen, he had thought then, were not supposed to take tips. Admittedly the song was just a fantasy, but still, it did not seem correct.

Penrose, he had learnt, had been obliged to follow up this roaring success with similarly mirthful other roles: including as a Laughing Curate, Golfer, Major, Typist and Lover. Imagine having to laugh on cue all the while, on stage, in the recording studio, and no doubt for your friends and fans too. Surely, thought Cogenhoe, sipping at a weak tea made from the dusty tea bags on the hospitality tray, this must be at the very least trying, and perhaps much worse. You must lose the ability to really laugh, in an unpremeditated way, to be caught joyously by something genuinely funny. He would not be at all surprised if Penrose had been, like many comics, secretly melancholy.

The collector had decided to say that he was in the town to research Penrose for an article and perhaps even a book. The performer's father, he knew, had been a watchmaker and jeweller here: the family had lived above the shop at Number 1, High Street, then in other places around the town as the business had prospered. And, since the story in the pamphlet was apparently also about Penrose, that would provide slyly the necessary link to ask about it. It could scarcely be about anything else, he thought, since nothing else seemed to happen here.

Cogenhoe had first been told about the elusive story by a collecting acquaintance of his, Michael Essendine, and he had been wary, sceptical even. This fellow was known to have a peculiar sense of humour, and sometimes invented things. It was even said that he spread news of fake rarities in order to distract attention from his quests for real ones. On the other hand, some of Essendine's tips had proved undoubtedly true, and timely. He had got Cogenhoe onto Fraser, for example, and Houghton, well ahead of the crowd, or at least the coterie, and so had enabled him to pick up their titles before they rose in value: no doubt only after he had got all *he*, Essendine, wanted, but even so. And the thing was, you could not risk missing out. Besides, Cogenhoe liked the chase, the game that was, at its best, like a detective story, and also in its way like an enigmatical supernatural story, a de la Mare or an Aickman, where you never quite knew where you were or what was to happen, or even what *had* happened.

Well, he certainly knew where he was now, he thought, as he put the vague tea in its blank white cup back onto the tray. In Biggleswade, Bedfordshire. It was time to explore, if that was not too grand a word for a perambulation of the predictable streets. He made his way down the stairs to the lobby, where the receptionist was studying a ledger and ignored him.

The clocks had gone back some time before and even though it was only early evening the dark had descended and the shops were closed. In the dimness of their various window displays he could see floral-decorated crockery, fawn corduroy jackets, faded magazines, gifts that nobody had chosen. The bustling wind seemed to encourage him along the High Street, though there was nowhere much beyond it that was worth more attention, so far as he could see. He stopped and cupped his hands to light a cigarette under the earnest glow of a streetlight. The fumes were seized and wafted away like a handkerchief in a conjurer's trick. He inhaled gratefully and considered what to do next. He ought to be after something in particular, he thought, to give his wanderings a goal, a purpose. Well, then, what was it that he ought to be after?

The likeliest places to find the pamphlet, if it was to be found, would be the library or a bookseller. He had no idea where either of these were, but at least he could now stalk the streets looking for them. On the other hand, it was to be presumed that other assiduous collectors had already tried these, so perhaps what he should really be looking for was the *unlikely* places. In his collecting he had sometimes found things where you would least expect them. At a shop in Radnorshire with rows of china dogs there had been a shed round the back with piles of damp books, well worth foraging in. In a supermarket foyer in a small Norfolk town there had been boxes of fat paperbacks on sale for local causes, but somebody had donated a dozen first editions of R. C. Hutchinson, a once-respected but now neglected author.

He remembered also a pub that had lined its walls with old books bought by the yard simply to give a quaint effect. He had not been able to resist studying them, of course. And there had been a Francis Brett Young title, not a particularly scarce one, but even so. He had said to the young waiter who had brought their food, "Do you mind if I steal one of your books?" The haughty youth had not been discountenanced: "I could not condone it, sir," he had replied. Cogenhoe had enjoyed the Jeevesian phrase, and repeated it to himself now, with a gentle laugh. And so he hadn't got the book, though it would not have been missed. He himself could not condone it either, he had found.

Where were the unlikely places here then? Well, you couldn't work it like that. The very point of the unlikely places was that you didn't expect them. They were only found by chance, by putting yourself in a slightly abstract state of mind, wandering around as it were aimlessly, giving chance a chance. So that is what he would do. And he would let his thoughts drift too.

The ash from his cigarette flew in fragile grey specks, and the wind seized his coat flaps, blowing them out like beige wings. Penrose, he now remembered, had been interviewed in the 1930s and, contrary to Cogenhoe's own theory that he must be lugubrious from all that laughing, had seemed quite contented and still fond of his home town. Still, that might have been just the public façade.

Penrose had been apprenticed to his father's clock and watch trade and remembered in particular an eccentric old lady whose grandfather clock he used to repair and maintain. It was her habit to go about the town with a wheelbarrow and, when she felt like it, to set this down and sit on it. She would then commence a lively patter of jokes and commentary, followed by a swirl of dancing and some boisterous singing: passers-by would give her money, though she did not ask for it. Perhaps her example, that had caused good-natured laughter to echo through the streets of Biggleswade for some years, had influenced Penrose to earn his own living from comic repartee and song. She was a "character". She had also been superstitious, especially when the clock stopped unexpectedly: there was a suggestion of the fortune-teller, even of the sorceress, about her.

The wind had now risen further and there was a spattering of rain in it too, which rattled rhythmically. A shred of newspaper scampered like a creature across the street, wrapped itself around his shins for an instant, and then darted off, as if expecting him to chase after it in some happy game. He stared at it, wondering if he should. He rather wanted to. And—there was a sudden lunge in his thoughts—had it been, definitely been, just a piece of newspaper? Could it have been a pamphlet? The thing was still tumbling down the street, alternately seen in gloom and amber as it passed into and out of the beams from the street lights. Every so often it would pause, caught in something, or resting in some temporary lull in the wind, but to Cogenhoe it seemed as if it was waiting for him, summoning him, daring him to join in its race.

It was absurd. Of course, it wasn't a pamphlet, and certainly not *the* pamphlet. It was just some bit of yesterday's paper that had leapt out of a waste bin or been thrown down by a loafer after he had studied the racing pages, or detached itself from fish and chip wrappings. It was being followed now, he saw, by scutterings of gold, copper and bronze leaves in an insistent susurrus like half-concealed sniggers, no doubt at his own delusions. And they were not pamphlets either, though they were strangely paper-like. After all, what colour was the cover of the pamphlet? He did not know. Was he quite sure they were all leaves?

He shook himself. It was time to go back. Tomorrow he would conduct proper research, get at the facts. That was what mattered. He would interview the librarian, find out what civic societies there were, or had been, go and see their secretaries. There was the town clerk, the bookshop proprietor, the postmaster or postmistress, the history teacher at the local school. One of them must know something. Thoroughness, that was it, a calm, careful, logical approach. By the time he left he would know for sure. Either it was there or it did not exist. And of course he would question them about old Penrose too, to keep up the idea of the supposed reason why he was there. Maybe even about that eccentric old lady also, to show he had already done his background work. Besides, she was interesting. There was something there, about the way Penrose had told of her, that hinted there was more to be told. The same could be true of the town itself. Could any place that could harbour two such curious individuals really be so prosaic? He laughed softly to himself as he thought of a pamphlet that he could produce, with some such title as *Secret Biggleswade*. Well, why not?

But as he made to turn, he found that the strong gusts caught him and carried him, not quite against his will, along the road. And everything else seemed in movement too. A bin lid clanged in the gutter ahead of him as if a mad cymbalist was marching about, shrubs swayed like green drunkards, and there was a roaring like a never-ending chant. The town, that he had thought so trim, seemed to squirm: the houses and shops were like rippling painted banners. And ahead, just at the farthest distance that he could see, there was still the pale shape of the piece of paper, gilded now by a light that seemed brighter than any streetlamp could cast.

Then he found himself spreading his arms wide and letting the wind fill his sails, and he joined his roar to the wind's roar.

It came to Cogenhoe, when he let himself go fully into the gale, that this was life as it should be, this wild rush, this hectic dash, this exhilaration, this ecstasy. His spirits soared with the wind, and he wanted to run with it forever, panting, joyous, heedless of where he was going or what happened next, hoping in fact that there was no next, except this and this and this. And as he ran, he heard, through the booming, a great laughter, over and over, a whooping, swooping, cacophony of bellows and guffaws, laughter, laughter, laughter, laughter ever after.

The Readers of the Sands

Three travellers headed by their different ways to a causeway leading them to the house called Driftwood End, which stood on a spur of land above a vast canvas of sand. Below, rotting, sea-whittled timber, old brindled ship's rope, rusting shards of iron, and the broken stone fangs of an ancient jetty littered the deserted shore. A fading red and white lifebelt, attached to a leaning post, was a reminder that the sands, which sometimes reached to the far horizon, could also soon succumb to the fast-surging sea.

There is only one refuge from the raging waves in those high tides, a single outcrop, quite far out, called the Lantern Isle. Here there had once been, in the last century, a hermit in a crude stone hut, accompanied by a cat and a goat. He kept a light ablaze at night, or when there was a fog, to warn the unwary. At times he would go ashore and sell prophecies, handwritten on any old scraps of paper, from door to door in the fishing villages and at the farms, and the small proceeds from these were almost sufficient to meet his needs. Though he was long since gone, perhaps some of his prophecies were still kept. A single red automatic blinking device, like some wakeful beast's eye, now warned mariners from the rock instead.

The first to arrive at Driftwood End came by foot, carrying a silver-tipped staff, which glinted as he strode. Mr. Hildreth was the latest holder of an ancient office. By long tradition, many rights over all the great expanse of the bay belonged to the church, and this included the right to traverse it from one headland to another. It was a journey of some six or seven miles and beset by difficulties—sudden streams, queachy expanses that sucked underfoot, and strands of slime, of sodden seaweed, that were treacherous when stepped upon. Only a sure guide knew the way around all of these hazards and could follow a true route on firmer sand, as well as knowing what diversions to take if sudden changes in the terrain should occur.

That guide, appointed after some years of study under a predecessor, took the title of the Bishop's Sandman and was able to collect a toll from all who took the journey across the estuary. In former times this had been a necessity, for the alternative way round the coastline was long and tortuous and lonely. Now the way across the sands was taken more as an adventure, an unusual ramble, accompanied at intervals by the recitation of legends and romantic history. But the solemn office was taken no less seriously for that. Mr. Hildreth had finished the two crossings, there and back, for this day and now made his way to the house at the end of the causeway. He had a trim white forked beard and quizzical white eyebrows which were in contrast to his brown weatherbeaten face, like a well-bletted fruit, and his eyes were pale blue, as if from long looking at the light of the sky on the horizon.

The second guest had commandeered the only cab at the lonely station a few miles away, and rode in it for as long as the track was passable, sighing as she alighted to complete the remaining few hundred yards herself. This was Madame Thebes, the seer, whose notices promising insights into fate and fortune, in return for a modest subvention, were to be seen in certain periodicals. Unusually, she did not use the cards or the stars or the palms to foretell things: she used sand, and patterns in the sand. She had the advantage, for her chosen profession (or perhaps it had chosen her, as she liked to aver), of an uncommon appearance, though most who met her would be hard put to say in what that consisted. There was something awry in the cast of her features, something aslant about her glance (from deep dark eyes) and some allure in her sad smile, that suggested the possessor of an unusual soul. This aside, all about her was quite precise and conventional: she did not affect flowing robes or talismanic jewels, but wore a well-cut tweed suit, with a neat scarlet and green neck-scarf clasped by a subtle onyx brooch. The effect of sober reliability was finished by her burnished brown brogues that now trod fastidiously towards the steps of the house at the crest of the road.

The Bishop's Sandman had already been ushered into the shore room, with its great windows overlooking the bay. It was faintly warmed by a fitful fire, muttering and whispering to itself and occasionally throwing up reluctant green-tinged saltwood flames. The visitor busied himself for a few moments in consulting the fine barometer made by Messrs Negretti & Zamba of Holborn Viaduct, which was fixed to the wall by the window. It was in transit from fair to unsettled, or from unsettled to fair, it was hard to tell which. Trusting his own precise instrument, his eyes, the better, he next gazed over the sandy expanse, noticing the beginnings of silvering in the wan sky.

There was a bustle at the door, and the second guest was shown in, and introduced herself. After pleasantries about the journey, there seemed hardly very much else to say, so they both looked out of the window a while. Then Madame Thebes enquired, "Do you know our host well?"

Hildreth stroked his white whiskers before replying.

"I can't say that I do. He has hired me at times to take him across the sands on various old paths, and we have spoken a little, but I would hardly say I know him."

"He goes looking for birds, I suppose?"

"Not birds, particularly, no, though he notices them."

"Flotsam and jetsam?"

"Not that either, though he will pick up whatever curious things the sea leaves behind."

The prophet was at a loss. "Seaweed?" she ventured. She had heard that some faddists gathered and ate this for their health. She hoped not here: she had an orthodox appetite, and did not relish the thought.

"No. I think—" the old guide paused, as if not sure whether to share his views. "I think he goes to look for traces in the sand."

Madame Thebes smiled. The effect, from her profusely powdered face, was rather as if a mummy had smirked.

"Does he now?" she replied. That would account, then, for her own unexpected invitation here, at a generous remuneration.

Her own prognostications were made by the casting of sand-grains over a book, as she had learnt they did in Thebes, or by the shaking of sand in a tray, as they did it in Marrakesh. There had once been a vogue for a book and a film called *The Garden of Allah*, enormously popular: a sand-seer featured in it, and she had long ago discerned the opportunity to present herself as England's only practitioner of the art. The novelty of it had borne her craft aloft for quite some time, and then she had only to maintain interest with startling, if well-nuanced, forecasts, and the judicious selection of testimonials from those beguiled by her work. Yet what was it her host wanted her to find here? She had no doubt that would soon appear.

"Are we the only two, do you think?"

"There is one other, I believe."

She subsided into silence. A rival? Perhaps. Well, they would work something out together, she was sure. The profession always had its ways.

The third arrival was in fact cycling slowly along the track towards the causeway, carefully avoiding its many furrows and holes, for she had in her knapsack an example of her art. Rachel Brown made hour-glasses and egg-timers out of carved sea-wood and blown glass, with fine tinted mineral sands to measure the passing of moments. Finding that too few people wanted these for practical purposes, she began to sell them as aids to quiet contemplation, a way of "watching the silence".

It was while practising this gentle rite herself, that she had noticed, at first incredulously, and then with growing wonder and certainty, her ability to still the sand, if only momentarily. She would watch the golden or green powder fall softly from one glass bulb to the other, she would stare at it intently and, just fleetingly, she found she could bring it to a halt. It could certainly be some hesitation in the flow of the grains, caused by a clustering, or a coarseness of the silt: it could be that. But it also seemed as if these tremors happened at her will, when she made them. She had said no word of this to anyone, for it troubled her slightly.

For the past few weeks she had been crafting what she called a study-glass for her host at Driftwood End, and he had invited her, while delivering it, to stay over with some other guests and explain to him how she created such pieces. As the day waned, she drew up her wheels at a point where a break in the walls and hedges that ran along the causeway gave out to a sweeping view. The sea was still far out, and the vista, framed by wind-wracked trees, was of a plain of sand, faintly rippled, predominantly dun-coloured or tawny, but with glimmers of silver and gold where the dim light caught it.

As she gazed, she saw a figure in a long dark coat, and a tilted hat, making across the shoreline in her direction, steadily. She thought of waving, but decided to wait until he should be within hailing distance. Perhaps he did not know that he should be keeping a keen eye for the first surge of the sea, and ensuring that he had time to scramble up to safety. She turned her attention from him and looked further out again, but there was no sign yet of the tide's coming.

As he neared, she called: "Hullo! Are you for the house?"

He looked up, halted, and took off his hat, the wind catching strands of his hair, the colour of hazel-wood.

"I am."

She beckoned him up to the haven of her lookout point, and he picked his way briskly over the rocks and between the thorns towards her. As he neared, she saw that he carried a slim leather cylinder strung over his shoulder. He hauled himself up by tussocks of grass and a broken fence to the track where she stood, and they looked at each other for a brief interval.

He had a sharp skull, with the weathered skin stretched tight across it, and brown flecked eyes like sea-washed pebbles. He affected a short, curt moustache.

"Philip Crabbe," he murmured, and proffered his hand.

"Oh," she said, "you ordered this hour glass from me. It's good of you to ask me to stay too. You said there'd be a small party of us?"

He nodded, but did not say more. Then they both gazed out over the bay. She wondered if it was a spyglass he carried, and why he didn't train it over the view before them.

"It's as well you came up here" she mentioned, "it must be about the turn of the tide soon and it's easy to get caught out. But I expect you know all about that."

He turned to her. "Yes, thank you. I've almost been caught once or twice, it's true. I'd have found a way up somehow, but . . . " and his words trailed away, before he found what he wanted to say, "but I was finding the shapes of the sands so fascinating, it was hard to draw away."

They started to walk towards the house, to the ticking of the wheels of her bicycle. After a slight deviation in the road, Crabbe's home came into view. It was made of speckled white stone which resembled the sand when it was at its driest and most sun-bleached, and in shape it was not unlike the sandcastles children make upon the beach. The greater part of it was a solid-looking, slightly tapering cylinder, as if cast from an upturned bucket, with windows in a neat column like glinting buttons on some great smock or coat. Lesser forms clustered against this staunch tower: a tall porch at the front, and (just to be seen) a long low tongue projecting out over the last of the spur on which the whole edifice stood: this was the shore room. A rock-wall and a grove of cypress trees, like green candle flames, were all the protection that the house had from whatever might be driven at it from out of the sea.

After they had dined, Philip Crabbe and his three guests gathered in the shore room, under the glow of lamps. It felt to Rachel Brown as if this furthest reach of the house, standing over the shore, was a refuge, the last citadel of human craft before the desolate elements. The impression was heightened by a wind rising outside, with a soaring sound.

Their host seemed at first diffident about the reason for his invitations. The talk over the meal had been general, touching on the locality and its flora and fauna, and on its legends, and on the changes the house witnessed as the seasons passed. Rachel had gathered a little about the others, and saw at once that they had in common the handling of sand. And, in view of his remark to her, Rachel was waiting for him to say a little more about what he meant. At length, as the conversation began to dwindle, and they all fell silent under the roaring of the wind, Crabbe reached for the tube he had been carrying, unfastened it, and gently eased out a roll of papers. He spread the maps and drawings out on the table, placing grey pebbles at each corner to hold them in place, and moved a lamp so that the amber light fell upon the sheets. This illuminated great swirls delineated in fine pencil strokes.

"This is a chart of the sands," he said, adding, "I made it myself. As I've walked across them at the lowest tide I've observed recurring markings, barely visible really, like the watermarks in the pages of a book: shapes made by the wind and the sea, and perhaps by some other influence we cannot see. This is what I've tried to map."

He paused here, as if thinking over the image he had just suggested.

"The fact is that these marks seem to me to suggest some sort of pattern. When I look at their silvery traces it's as if they are paths in a labyrinth, and I sometimes think that if I followed them I might be led towards—well, a kind of clarification. Of a mystery whose nature I do not yet know. I'm afraid I cannot put it any better than that."

In the silence that followed his hesitant remarks, the hollow roaring of the wind seemed to encroach further into the room, booming in the chimney and rattling the casements. The flames in the fireplace writhed in a green and golden saraband.

"I've asked each of you here," Crabbe continued, after the pause had lasted for several solemn minutes, "because it seems to me that you each in your way have some affinity with sand, with the way sand shapes and moves, a sort of sensitivity. I want your advice: I want to know if you see in the shapes of the sands out there"—he gestured to the window at the bay beyond—"what I have begun to see. I won't say too much more, because I don't want to influence your response. I recognise . . . " He paused awkwardly. "I am asking you to take part in a sort of experiment, I suppose, and I don't quite know where it will lead. If you'd rather not . . . "

None of his three guests took the opportunity for release he offered. For Madame Thebes it was all part of the trade, for the Bishop's Sandman it was not his code to leave a man in stormy waters, and Rachel Brown felt a keen affinity with the mystery Crabbe was so hesitantly outlining.

"Well, I thank you. To begin, would you each please have a look at my chart and form your impressions? Take your time."

The three visitors leant over the unfurled paper on the table, each keeping their breathing light as if their exhaling might disturb the frail sand patterns delineated there. The delicate stipple of Crabbe's diagrams seemed to hold an inner light under the glow of the lamp. There was the faintest rippling in the paper from some freshet of air feeling its way into the room, the last reach of the high winds without. It was as if the markings wanted to make their meanings known, to impress themselves upon those in the room.

Just like a séance really, thought Madame Thebes. She settled herself comfortably to allow any inspiration to occur to her about what exactly Crabbe wanted. Sometimes when she did this, she was surprised to find that things surfaced in her thoughts which were not worked out by her, but seemed to come from elsewhere, and this often made her think that maybe she did have "the sight" or something like it after all.

Mr. Hildreth felt uneasy. He was an outdoor man, who liked the direct experience of the sun, the rain and the wind, and did not relish looking at interpretations of things, though he appreciated the usefulness of maps. But out of politeness he allowed his gaze to linger over the charts, following in his imaginations routes across them.

Rachel Brown found herself beguilingly drawn to the precise yet somehow elusive stipple before her. It was meticulously set out yet it did not seem to her to quite cohere, as if the pencil marks might easily be brushed or blow from the page, or might indeed decide to re-form themselves into shapes other than those Crabbe had delineated.

"The sands know their own way," at length commented Mr. Hildreth, as if echoing her thoughts. "We can study them, as I do every day, but we can never be sure of them."

Philip Crabbe nodded.

"But I wonder what their way is?" he murmured.

Beyond the windows the wind whistled, as if its soaring was seeking the same answer.

Madame Thebes thought that this might be the right moment.

"The sands know more than we can say," she began, and was about to go on with a variation on the usual patter to her readings, when she found other words coming through her instead. "The images are in them. The images make use of them. They make use of us too, but it is the sands that know their form most. The sea and the sand and the wind together are expressions of them. We are not meant to see them, Mr. Crabbe. We are meant to shiver in the wind and feel our souls surge at the sea and gaze at the sands as at infinity, but that is as close as we should be. We are not to know more. No more."

The last words seem to have a studied ambiguity. Know more or no more? She was not sure herself if they were a conclusion or a contradiction. She relapsed into silence, surprised at herself, at what she had said. It almost made too much sense.

Crabbe was staring at her intently. Well, she thought, returning more to her usual self, he's getting his money's worth. But she found that she was drifting again, could no longer keep a focus on the mannerisms of her craft. Instead of watching to see what he might want next, trying to divine sympathetically what best to say, she felt the remembrance of the words coming back to her and it was all she could do to stop more words coming. And there began to come to her with an awful certainty a single phrase. It rose in her just as the wind rose from the sands outside. She tried to hold it back, to stay still and stolid, but it was no good and the words soon burst out of her.

"The images are here!"

And she found herself staring wildly about her, as if she might see them in all their awful glory. The young woman next to her put a pale hand upon hers, and it steadied her a little. But she remained brittle. She hated it when things really came to her like this and she could no longer control them.

Mr. Hildreth cleared his throat, got up abruptly from the table and went to stare out of the window again. Madame Thebes looked at him. That's no good, she thought, they are out there too and that's more where they ought to be, where they belong. He might be expert at negotiating them during the day but he really knows nothing of the night. But in this she soon saw she was not quite right.

"Sometimes," he said, "I think I see things on the horizon. Islands that aren't there. Mirage, of course. Effect of haze. And yet in that moment, I don't know. You could imagine going there, somehow. Similar in the mist. Shapes. Never do quite work out what they are. Or who they are, I suppose. But you feel as if you ought to go towards them and find out. Don't know if it all means anything."

He looked back into the room. The trio were very still, as if they had been preserved in an oil painting, an effect which the quiet lamp light and the glimmering upon a silver coffee pot enhanced. There was a lustre too upon the beautiful hour-glass the young woman had made, which was displayed on the table. It was not clear that they had heard him. In the dimness he tried to look into the glitter of their eyes. Crabbe's were withdrawn, almost somnolent, the fortune-teller's were active, furtive, restless, and the young woman's had a fierce concentration. This would not quite do, he thought. The guide in him decided to lead them out of this too. He stretched out an arm as if to show the way. But as he did so he seemed to catch sight of a shape in the distance of the long room that was like those he sometimes saw when he was crossing the sands. It was no more than a gathering of greyness. He thought to himself that it was like a coat hanging on a hat-stand, but of course there was no hat-stand. It did not move, it was as if it was always there but only now could be seen. And he found himself unable to do anything other than stand there and stare at it.

Crabbe knew that they were in the room too, the silver shapes that he saw upon the shore in his long walks. They were like the slim arrows of rain caught in their falling.

He had to look at them aslant because he knew they must not be seen in all their light. Even then, this was only their semblance, not their essence, which was not to be comprehended. He was exultant at what he knew, but thought, with a surge of self-reproach, that he had been wrong to pull these others into it too. But a comfort came, in that perhaps they also had been meant to have this glimpse: after all, they all admitted they knew something of it already. Or did they all? The young woman—had she said, or had he only guessed? He stole a glance at her. She seemed composed, concentrating. He tried to offer a nod of reassurance but her gaze was fixed elsewhere.

Madame Thebes was trying hard not to look at anything for very long. It was enough that the words were still in her, the words that had told that the images were there with them. What they were exactly she did not want to see, for she had known them when they took over her tongue. But then it began to seem to her as if she were falling, falling, like that surge of unconsciousness that comes to us when we feel sleep coming but have not quite gone there yet. She was both surrendering her self-possession and yet also knew this was what she was doing and did not want to give it up. It was like descending a long steep dark chute.

And Crabbe knew it too. To him it was like those times when he had heard the distant roar of the tides coming in and knew he must get to the shore without delay. But now the waves were almost upon him, and he knew that he must succumb. The silvery glinting from the figures he had glimpsed was dispersed among the sea-spray in a myriad of shining facets that were going to rise above him and overcome him. Along with their fierce light there was a vast coldness coursing through all his veins, his very bones.

The Bishop's Sandman had found that as he watched the grey form it seemed to seep into himself. He felt the motes of ash become him, hover within. His own lean figure was suspended and this was taking its place. It was as if he had seen a shape in the mist and gone towards it and found that when he came up to it they had merged. And what there had been of him was no longer there, only a shade that seemed to twist in and out of existence. He knew this was happening but he had no volition to prevent it.

When Rachel Brown heard Madame Thebes pronounce the immanence of the images, she knew at once what she meant, and knew also that she was right. She felt the woman's surge of fear and put out a hand to console her. And she knew also with a quick inrush of certainty that she must crystallise her mind. At once her thoughts went to her study-glass, a favourite, in all the strange elegance of its carved wood and its curved glass. It was one she had worked on with a fierce fascination, feeling it take fastidious shape under her fingers. It was presently still, and she focused her attention upon it, and seemed to see every individual bead of sand within as if it were a tiny jewel, radiant with bright colours. She reached out and turned the instrument gently over. As she watched, the grains began to fall into the lower receptacle, in a silent glimmering. And to her it was as if she knew each one, its particularity, its iridescence and its prismatic light, its own curious form.

She heard the others about her in the room shift in their places, was aware of their troubled responses, but knew that she must concentrate on the beautiful glass in both her outer and inner gaze. The shining grains were falling freely now and it came to her also that she must try to make them falter, to halt however briefly in their natural flow. This was no longer the curious, slightly light-hearted whim of before, the desire to just see what she could do. She knew that a high, urgent entreaty had attached itself to the idea. It was no longer a game, if it had ever been: her power was needed. But this knowledge made her task much harder. It made her, for a moment, waver, and the sand sped on through its narrow course. She thought she had lost her affinity with the flowing forms and had to struggle to resume her knowledge of them. And now it was time to make them stop, to intercede a pause.

She angled her mind at them and tried. As she did so, she felt an overwhelming rush of forces course through her. There was in succession a sense of falling, a great coldness, a dissolving, and at once she became intensely aware of her companions in the room and of the wind keening beyond. There was the slightly awry face of Madame Thebes, the taut visage of Philip Crabbe, the weathered flesh of Mr. Hildreth, all caught in the glows and the hollows of the lamplight as if in a tableau. Their hands did not move but it seemed to her that they reached out to her all the same. She *must* make the grains stop if only for the merest of moments. Only in that faltering, she knew, could the three before her elude the knowledge of the images.

The presence of the work she had made, the precious craft, the study-glass in all its fine shape and feel, had never quite left her, and she fought back against the disorienting forces that had come upon her, to bring it into focus once more. Then the beads of sand seemed to dance before her once more and she allowed herself to gaze upon their scintillant joy. The turning away to those beside her had been only for a moment, though it had felt longer, and the flow through the delicate funnel was still following its ordained way. She stared hard at the glass and the grains within, and thought she saw them slow, and gave them again all her fierce attention. They faltered, flickered, and in a moment like a great descent of silence, they halted and they held. And she knew that it was enough, that she had opened a moment when the images were no longer there, when those who were there with her could be spared their knowledge of them. Their figures stirred, they were like sleepers in armchairs roused from an afternoon slumber. But as for her, she had known the gulfs of the great silence: and her fierce face was white and defiant.

The Understanding of the Signs

But why the Red Lion? And why the White Hart, and the Black Horse, and the Green Dragon? The mystery of English inn signs has interested me since I was young. I collected pub names on family journeys and even issued a typed newsletter on the subject. I liked the fabulous beasts and the painted signboards depicting them in fierce glory. There are books that seek to explain them but they are never very convincing. I began to look into them and in most cases the supposed explanation fell apart when you looked at it closely.

The signs can't always be linked to local landed gentry or aristocrats. I thought of them as similar to the monsters and grotesques you find carved in wood and stone in churches. Though these are sometimes thought to typify vices, in many cases the precise vice is by no means obvious and in any case the gusto with which they were made rather belied the suggestion. I had a hazy theory that there was a sort of common bestiary, a folk heraldry of strange hybrids that the craftsmen liked to create and the people enjoyed. They were evidently archetypes which, although seemingly not seen in nature, had a lively existence in the collective imagination.

Of course, some pub names *are* straightforward—the Railway, the New Inn, and so on—and some of those that seem old are in fact fairly recent titles simply adopted because they sound traditional. Nevertheless, there is a rich region of research and speculation here, and compared to, say, churches, the history of old pubs and their signs hasn't had very much critical, scholarly attention.

When I started looking into the matter, I found there was one venerable authority, Jacob Larwood and John Camden Hotten's *A History of Signboards* (1867), revised as *English Inn Signs* (1951) by Gerald Millar, and a few modern commentators, but mostly of the "quaint customs" variety. One exception to this was Sam Wildman's *The Black Horsemen: English Inns and King Arthur* (1971), a wonderfully imaginative but rather improbable study linking the Black Horse sign to battles and campaigns connected with the Dark Age warlord's cavalry. But at least this author was putting forward something new and unusual, and he was right at least in this, that we really don't know a lot about where exactly pub names came from: and some may have unexplored links to folklore and legend.

I later found two other interesting books on English inn signs. *The Spotted Dog: A Book of English Inn Signs* (1948) by Reginald Turnor, with wood engravings by John Farleigh, which I found in an antiques barn in Babylon, Ely. This is a diffuse, not to say languorous, study which sticks mostly to the acknowledged interpretations and is therefore quite a good guide to the conventional view of these. He takes us through religious signs derived from pilgrims' hostels to heraldic signs from royal or aristocratic coats of arms to trade and agricultural signs and on to those named after eminent people, ending with a chapter on the more unusual and inexplicable signs, and possible explanations for these.

Even Mr. Turnor, however, is struck by some aspect of ungraspability in the imagery of inn signs and how they relate to history, lore, and landscape. In his very last sentence he says, "So I say again that the inn sign is a clue, a key, a starting-point in the search for an essence—the traditional pattern of England."

However, *The Rising Sun: A Study of Inn-Signs, Volume 1* by H. T. Sherlock (1937: no further volumes seem to have been published) is a complete contrast to the Turnor book: it departs radically from the conventional explanations in favour of a single overarching and highly individual theory. "This book deals with the origin of the earliest signs. It shows the relation of the inns with ancient pilgrimage, with the village Wakes, with May Day festivities, with rites for the fertility of the field and with worship of sun and fire. Folk-lore, folksong and folk-custom all contribute to the understanding of the signs," we are told.

Helen Sherlock considers that many inn signs derive from ancient solar worship and its associated rituals and mysteries, and devotes much ingenuity to showing that even unobvious signs are really sun symbols. There can be little doubt, as Turnor also recounts, that some inns were halts on pilgrim routes, and we should not underestimate how important pilgrimages were in medieval times. But this book goes even further back, invoking Osiris and the Egyptian mysteries, and suggests that pubs were often stations or gates on the journey to the west. It is all most splendid and in a strange sort of way almost persuasive: you end up thinking there must be something in it. My favourite bit is the idea that the sign of the Cat & Fiddle is really the cat-goddess Baast and her sistrum.

Though it may seem highly speculative, I would rather have this strange, mysterious and arcane book than any more measured and sceptical study, simply because Helen Sherlock seems to hover so close to the hidden dimensions of inn sign symbolism. Nor is she alone. In Arthur Machen's *The Great Return*—the return is of the

Holy Grail—the two pubs in the little harbour town of Llantrisant are called "The Crown" and "The Fisherman's Rest", a sly allusion to the Fisher King, the focal figure of the Grail legends.

In modern times, the two things we can say with certainty about English pubs are that many of them are being closed and many others are having their names changed. This question of changing the name of a thing is often thought in folklore to be inadvisable. Mariners did not like it in relation to ships, and the same has been said about house names, as instanced occasionally in Shirley E. Peckham's *Unusual British House Names and their Origins* (1988). A sequel, *No. 13: unlucky/lucky for some, a book describing the real life experiences of over 350 people living in houses numbered thirteen or having some other connection with number thirteen* (1994) by Shirley E. Peckham and Prabhakar G. Bhagwat suggests that not only names but numbers should not be changed.

Not so long ago I encountered one who was very firmly of this view too, particularly in relation to lost pubs. I have already indicated a certain tendency amongst amateur scholars of inn signs towards the, shall we say, speculative, as seen in the works of Wildman and Sherlock. But this inclination is by no means over. It was my good fortune to make the acquaintance of a reclusive scholar who had devoted himself to this field of study for some years.

I had written a checklist of the literature of terrestrial zodiacs (which are another matter), which is often fugitive and ephemeral. Many accounts of them originally appeared only in obscure booklets, now fragile and fading, and printed in small numbers, or in similar arcane journals. So I had been compiling the first attempt at a full bibliography of this curious subject, in which I identified around thirty examples of possible zodiacs in the literature.

This work had appeared in various journals and it was through one of these that I made contact with A. M. Whetstone. He told me that there was another aspect of the whole matter which I had not touched upon, and he would be glad to explain his discovery to me. There are indeed, he said, giant figures in the English landscapes, but they are not zodiacal signs, or at least not only these. They are the ancient archetypal beasts of these islands. Moreover, said he, there is a particular reason for paying attention to them just now.

Of course, I hastened to assure him of my interest, and after some correspondence he invited me to visit him in his digs, which were in the old Yorkshire town of Settle, a place which has several of those narrow alleyways between tall buildings which often bear local names—jitty or jetty, where I come from, snicket or ginnel in those parts. The door to Mr. Whetsone's abode was some way along one of these and led to several flights of stairs up to the top of the premises.

Partly because of his rather formal mode of address, I had supposed I was about to meet some aged, portly gentleman grown venerable in years of study. But the figure who greeted me following my knock at his door was still quite young, with a shock of scarlet hair and a keen, austere face. He ushered me in. The room was stuffed with books. They were not only vertical in the cases that lined all but one wall, they were horizontal too and at all angles, wherever they could be crammed in. It would be fair to say condition was evidently not one of Whetstone's concerns: the books were often tatty, faded, stained, and battered. The same could not be said of him: he was spruce, almost dandyish. The one wall that did not have books had instead a great wall chart depicting a map of England and Wales, and on these various emblems had been inked in jewelled colours, and lines and curves had been superimposed with blurred pencil strokes.

As sometimes happens when one meets a stranger, we began talking at once and roamed rapidly from subject to subject, each leading naturally to the other, without cease for several hours, except when he provided a pot of strong Nepalese tea and a plate of plain biscuits. At length we converged on the topic that had resulted in his invitation: the linkage between inn signs, zodiacs in the landscape, and ancient symbols. He explained that he had been following up a lot of curious hints and clues about the oldest inn signs and that he was pretty sure they began, as both Wildman and Sherlock thought, much further back.

"It is a very great mistake," said Whetstone, "to change the name of an inn."

I said I thought so too. The older names were better. And I mentioned the superstition.

"It isn't a superstition," said he. "It's a fact."

I asked him why he thought so.

"Well, let me ask you a question. What becomes of the lost signs?"

"Oh, well, I suppose they are scrapped. A few might be sold to collectors."

"No, no, but the symbol itself. The thing signified."

"I see. Well, it will be remembered for a while, no doubt, and then forgotten."

"*We* might try to forget, yes. But I tell you this. The signs remain. The lions, the horses, the unicorns, the dragons, the eagles, and the swans. They are still there. And they are displeased at their new neglect. Our—well, affinity, with them is diminished, you see. Now, they are loose in the world."

I said I thought this was an interesting idea, and he laughed bitterly. I could see that he was less confident in our shared interests at this point, and the talk became more desultory, but he invited me to see him again the following weekend and join him for a walk in the hills nearby. I met him in Settle, we fortified ourselves with his Nepalese tea, and then we set off. It was only when we drew up at a hollow in a narrow lane that he pointed upwards to our goal. It was some walk: up Pen-y-Ghent.

Now Pen-y-Ghent is not the highest hill in England by a long way, nor even in the Yorkshire Dales. But it is a prominent landmark, somewhat like some great crouching beast, and Whetstone explained that it has at least one unusual feature: it has retained its ancient name, its British name, in fact from the lost Cumbrian language which was akin to Welsh. No Anglo-Saxon or Norse name has replaced it and that in itself is, he said, significant. It suggests that the newcomers to the country did not care to meddle with it. "Pen" means head, he went on, as in Penzance, which means "Holy Head", and the rest of the name has been suggested to mean head of the winds, certainly plausible, though there are windier peaks nearby, or head of the border. But what border? To that I feel our experience might have helped to suggest a possible answer.

It was late afternoon by the time we scrambled to the top and stood by the trig point. Winds there certainly were here, and the cloud shadows moved over the fields and the fells, so that all the country below seemed to be rippling, now in the light, now in shadow. There was nobody else out about: and beneath the soaring of the air there was, as it seemed to me, a hollow silence. And it was into this silence that Whetstone started reading. Or reciting, chanting to be more exact, from a book. It was one of his most ragged and faded volumes and I later got a glimpse of its title, or thought I did: *Babylon's Handwriting*. But how could it be? Because that (as I knew from my own studies of seventeenth century sects) is a lost work by the prophet Lady Eleanor, who foretold the death of Charles I and thought that Oliver Cromwell was the saviour of the nation because his initials denoted the sun and the crescent moon. A waning moon, though, perhaps we should note.

"In the Discernings of Tinkers, the Merlinings, and the foresights, is display'd the Kingdom," I heard him chant, and then there was something about how the "Cloven-Footed flesh Becomes hot Scarlet", and "Mineral tongues Speak". "The Leopard's Eyes," he proclaimed, "Are Regents of the Fires, and The Scaly Ones soar: Time is pouring-out All, The Stones are unleash'd, The Great Horns roar In the shaken clouds."

I could hear the capital letters in his pronouncements.

"Beware the ravings of Draymen," he went on, "The Bloody Lion's paw, The caws of the Seven Crows" (all admirable injunctions), and there was quite a bit more.

I can't answer for the exact wording, and perhaps that is just as well. I've got some things muddled, no doubt. But that was the sort of flavour of it. And as he expounded this incantation, his eyes looked into mine: and it seemed to me as if the clouds were moving in his gaze too. I turned away, not quite sure what to do. I often think that English awkwardness at anything too mystical and fervoured might be a guard against the truly outlandish that is more powerful than bell, book, and candle.

But whether it was the uncanny effect of that glimpse of his eyes, or the curious influence of his chanted words, I found, when I began to look over the distant views to the far horizons, that the movement of the cloud shadows had become swifter and seemed to make all the land look alive. It was quickened with a fierce energy, and as I stared I seemed to see hints of limbs: wings, paws, talons, claws, a vast mane, a flickering tongue. Nothing cohered into a definite shape I could name, and yet I thought that this might transpire at any moment.

It was like looking at some great medieval tapestry but made in the very terrain itself, a tapestry that swayed and billowed in the wind. And I knew that I was seeing the stirring of the ancient bestiary of these isles, but for what purpose, with what intent, I did not know. Yet I did not think it boded well for us. There was a baleful power in the movement of these shadowy beasts that suggested nothing human counted for very much with them, now that we had begun to abandon them.

The gorse on the hills seemed to form golden shapes, the bare grey outcrops of rock gleamed silver, and in the roaring of the wind there was a deeper snarling. The contours of the hills, the sweeping slopes, were like palpitating flanks, the spurs of outlying ridges seemed to stretch out like paws. I shook my head several times, and wiped my eyes, and when I stared again for a few moments it seemed as though all these visions had gone: but then it all returned and I found I could not misinterpret what I was seeing. I crouched down and gestured to Whetstone to stop, but he either did not see or did not care and went on chanting.

After what seemed a very long time but later proved to be only a few minutes, the flow of the wind upon the hill and over its domain below seemed to slow and the images to diminish, and Whetstone's voice faded into silence too.

"You saw?" was all he asked, and I nodded.

"What the hell is in that tea of yours?" I asked, mild humour being another English resort in times of disturbance.

He smiled, but we made our way down the long track in silence. Before I left him that evening, I asked of course about the book. But he was diffident. It was a rag-bag, he said, of the old seer's sayings, an eighteenth-century scrapbook, given the title of Lady Eleanor's most noted work, but probably with not much originally hers in it. Yet, as he had found, it seemed to have a certain potency, though he thought other things might do just as well.

That was the last I saw of A. M. Whetstone. I had a note from him to say he was moving from his rooms in Settle further west, to seek for, as he put it, what was left of the old Cumbrian or Cymric tongue, and to find what might be seen from higher places still. I often wonder what glimpses he might have got from on top of Scafell or Helvellyn or, say, perhaps in some other high place altogether, some other boundary between the worlds.

Lost Estates

I was playing the trans-dimensional crumhorn when the man from the Treasury called. I put it aside reluctantly and let him in

"Thank you for agreeing to see me," he said. Possibly some of the echoes from the instrument, my own invention, were still lingering, because he looked about rather oddly. I ushered him to a chair and offered him a cup of tea, which he declined.

There was a pause.

I was still holding his business card, which was both impressive yet discreet. It bore a crown and a portcullis and his name, R. H. Asher, M.Sc. (Econ.) (St.) and the legend "Estates". I couldn't remember what "St." stood for. He could hardly be claiming to be a saint, not yet anyway. One of the new universities, perhaps: Stamford, Stevenage, Stranraer?

"I'm sorry," I said, "the person you wrote about doesn't mean anything to me. Not at all."

"So I understood, sir. But it is a matter of some importance to us, you see. Or else we wouldn't have bothered you. It's good of you to agree to see me."

"Well," I replied, obligingly, "I suppose there must be a good many people we each encounter as we go along, and we can't be expected to remember all their names, can we?"

But I had the impression that the man from the Treasury didn't forget. Ever. However, he nodded slightly, as if in sympathy. He was younger than I had expected and, even more surprisingly, wore his grape-dark hair quite long, curling around the nape of his neck.

"Perhaps if you told me the context?" I ventured.

"There is no context, really. Just a piece of paper with your name and address on it, in pencil. Quite old, not new. And not very much else to go on."

"No diary, address book, calendar, or, er, documents?" He shook his head sorrowfully.

"Well, were there any other names at all? Perhaps they might suggest a connexion. Mutual friends, acquaintances," I added vaguely.

Mr. Asher stirred, a bit uneasily I thought. Aha!

"There were: a few. But I can't very well tell you those, out of confidentiality, you see. Just as I wouldn't tell anyone else yours. Who wasn't official, I mean."

I didn't quite like the sound of that added reservation. In fact, the whole remark sounded a bit off to me, as if there might be something disreputable about my association with this stranger.

"Have you got a photograph?" I asked

"A photograph isn't available," he said. I thought this was cautiously worded.

"Could you tell me a little bit more about why you are interested in him?" I said, in admittedly a slightly brusque a tone. "That might help," I added, to sound more obliging.

"I don't think it will. But it's quite simple. We are looking into his estate. We have to try to find a next of kin, or similar."

"I see. It must be interesting work. If saddening, sometimes."

"It is. Both of those. Of course, finding him would be even better," he added, and then apparently regretted it.

I seized upon this. "How do you mean? Is he missing, presumed—?" And then I remembered this was a wartime phrase, and presumably didn't apply.

"I mustn't keep you on this occasion," he said hurriedly. "We have a number of other things to follow up. However, if we don't get anywhere, I wonder—?"

"Yes?"

"May I call again? Perhaps if you wouldn't mind telling me a little about your own background then, it might help. Something might crop up."

I wasn't very keen. I had my work to do. But my curiosity had been roused rather.

"Well, if you think it would help, then I suppose so."

As soon as I said this, I knew he would be back, whether or not his other enquiries led anywhere. And probably he would have come whether I had agreed or not.

When he had gone, I sat in thought for some time. I wanted to resume the trans-dimensional crumhorn, but I was feeling too bothered. I began to rummage in my old diaries, letter files, papers, cuttings, concert posters, as if the name I did not know would suddenly come to light. But it didn't. I began to think about all the different things I'd done that might have led to a passing contact with someone, in all sorts of different situations, and before long I felt as though I had been accused of something and had to find evidence to refute the charge, whatever it was. Then I tried to work out the various reasons why anyone might make a note of my name and address even though I did not know them. There was one obvious reason, the band, but that was a long time ago.

✳

Mr. Asher, M.Sc. (Econ.) (St.) came back, as I knew he would.

"Well," I said, trying to be light about it, "this estate must be worth a lot, for you to take so much trouble over it. I feel I ought to pretend to be the long-lost heir, to get my hands on it."

He regarded me gravely.

"We always take trouble, sir," he said. This sounded more like a threat than a placid customer service announcement.

"But alas, I cannot make any such claim. I still know nothing at all about him. No good at all, I'm afraid. I've looked in my papers, not a sign. I've thought about it quite a bit. Nothing. Sorry."

"It's sometimes better if you don't try too hard. To think about it."

"Yes, I know. But, of course, we may never have had any contact. Maybe he just heard of me from some mutual acquaintance."

"In which case, sir, we may have to think about which of your acquaintances that might be. But not yet."

He held up a hand as he saw that I was about to object.

"First," he resumed, "I would like to eliminate the obvious. You have not, I take it, had any involvement in the legal profession? No? Medical? Education? The Services? The Church, or anything similar?"

I shook my head to all of these, although I did wonder what "anything similar" might encompass, in relation to the Church. Maybe it had been similar, in some ways. I said nothing.

"Well, that clears the way a bit. Those are the sort of people, you'll agree, that anyone might be likely to have some contact with. Lawyer, doctor, soldier, teacher, priest. It sounds like a children's rhyme, doesn't it, sir. Next, do you buy or sell anything?"

I hesitated. "Not exactly."

"Inexactly, then."

I waved vaguely. "I make music. I suppose some people might buy it, but if so it's not obvious."

He nodded.

"What sort of music?"

"I was in The Perpetual Motion Machine Company," I admitted.

His face remained impassive.

Of course, he hadn't heard of us. But he inclined his head, as if respectfully.

"What did you play, sir?"

"All sorts. We all played everything."

"I see." He didn't. Nor did the music industry, unfortunately. We made one album and one EP and that was it. Of course, there were other projects.

"Doesn't get us very much farther, does it?" I notice I had said "us". So it was my mystery too, now, was it?

"Well, it all helps to build up a picture. I may need to share some more background with you, But I'll need to talk to someone else first. I'll be back in touch, I expect."

As he was at the door, he said: "And do you still play, sir?"

I nodded very slightly.

"Solo work?"

"Not exactly," I said.

"Any other members of the band still around? Any chance of a reunion?"

"They're around," I replied.

After he had gone, I began to wonder a bit about his exact role. There seemed to be something more here than settling lost estates. Too much effort going into it for that.

❋

The crumhorn is an instrument that is mostly used in hey-nonny-no bands that dress up in medieval costumes and perform in old churches and at Christmas markets. And it is deep and sonorous and, some say, a bit galumphing. But I like it, there's something about it that seems to speak of ancient aeons. I wouldn't be surprised if it suddenly decided to talk in prehistoric tongues. The trans-dimensional version was my own invention. Most of the things we played in The Perpetual Motion Machine Company were our own concoctions. They might start from a known instrument, but they struck out further, into unknown regions—the title, in fact, of our album.

In the case of the crumhorn, I had adapted it electronically with vast echo chambers and reverb so that its great groans were intensified, and sounded indeed like an antediluvian beast calling for its mate. Then I added my patent random noise generator, so that there was an impression it was coming over an obscure radio station broadcasting from a distant star, or a distant time, or both. I liked the effect of all this, but whether anyone else would was a moot point, so that was the title I had given to the slowly-evolving piece I was performing. It was fortunate that my studio flat was above a stuffed toy warehouse, as there was no-one below at night to complain, and no doubt the toys, and their crates and boxes and packaging, absorbed some of the noise. I did sometimes wonder if I might one day during a session hear a knock at the door and find several irate teddy bears fixing me with their amber glass eyes. I had wandered through the warehouse once and they did all seem to be staring balefully at me.

When I had replied that my current project was "not exactly" solo work, I was of course being a bit guarded. Most artists don't like to say too much about stuff in progress, because then some of the inspiration seeps out:

it has escaped, and you cannot always get it back. But that wasn't the only reason. The fact is that in composing and creating "Moot Point", I had sometimes encountered surprising sounds. Of course, my random noise generator was designed to do just that, but this isn't what I mean. I know the sort of thing it will offer: hisses, whooshes, bleeps and crackles. Excuse the technical terms here. But the unfamiliar sounds weren't any of those. They were more like hollow roars and wailing winds.

After Mr. Asher had gone, I didn't feel like resuming work. I was baffled both by him and the persistence of his mission and by this stranger who had written my name and address down some time ago. It's true I had occasionally received letters out of the blue about the group, usually asking if I could help them find the LP or EP which, I gathered, now changed hands for a tidy sum among certain cognoscenti. We could have done with some of that at the time. That was probably the likeliest explanation: another collector of recorded arcana. Even so, I began to feel uneasy and to go over incidents and encounters in my past that might stir the authorities' interest in me. I even began to wonder whether this was all a cover story, and they were actually investigating me, not the supposed "lost estate" or missing person, or whatever it was. But that was, of course, quite ridiculous. Next I had suspicions about whether R. H. Asher M.Sc. (Econ.) (St.) was who he said he was. I had, after all, only seen his business card, and before that there had just been a telephone call to make the appointment. He didn't look like a civil servant, still less a Treasury official, with his nape-length hair and, now I came to think of it, rather foppish collar and cuffs. Not that I could object on those grounds, since my own style has been described as like an exiled Maharajah fallen on hard times. Still, it was odd in a Whitehall man.

Then it occurred to me that I didn't know where this chap, the stranger I mean, lived. He knew where I lived, he had written it down, got it from somebody, presumably. (Who? I didn't exactly have a teeming social circle.) But Asher hadn't mentioned it. Presumably it came under his heading of "confidentiality". Yet it might help. If I knew where they came from, that might nudge a thought. I resolved to take up the point with him next time he called, which I had no doubt he would.

But in fact there was a long gap before I heard from him again, and that wasn't at my flat. I didn't like this silence. I felt left in limbo. It was like going to one of those parties where somebody you've hardly met puts their head at an angle, eyes you carefully, and says, "You know, you're really rather—" and then some description you would never apply to yourself, so that you wonder about it afterwards and still can't make it out, and never meet them again, and so never do. I remembered that Asher had said he had to talk to someone else before he could give me any more background, and I surmised that this was the cause of the delay. Perhaps they didn't agree to this. Or perhaps they had found out all about the stranger and no longer needed me, and hadn't bothered to tell me.

It had been a few years since the three of us (there was an occasional fourth) in The Perpetual Motion Machine Company had met, and I began to wonder about getting in touch. We had never, by the way, broken up, more faded away, due to lack of interest. But I had heard of some bands who had not got very far in their time, but were now almost fêted, at least by an earnest, questing minority. Perhaps we should give it a try. And they might recognise the name that I didn't. I tried Triff first. That was what we called her because she was always saying it when a piece or a performance went well: "Triff!"

We did the usual catching-up and reminiscing stuff, then vaguely talked about wouldn't it be wonderful if, and have you heard from, and well let's think about it, keep in touch, when Triff said, just as the call seemed to be petering out:

"I've had such an odd man come round to see me a couple of times."

"Oh, yes?" I said. "A fan?"

But I already knew, of course. So I told her he had been to see me too, and then we both wondered some more between us. Triff didn't recognise the name either. Obviously, the fact that we were both involved, apparently, made it obvious that The Perpetual Motion Machine Company was the connecting link. But then it emerged, when we compared notes, that he had only visited her after the second time he saw me, presumably following up my passing mention of the band. This was getting murkier.

We agreed to meet and maybe have a bit of a jam, and Triff said she would ask Mix, our third member. We called him that because he liked to spend a lot of time on the mixing desk, and because whenever we veered off course he'd just say "all goes in the mix". To complete the picture, I suppose I ought to admit that my name in the band was Ink because, well, I'm writing this, aren't I? I did all the band's paper-work and kept records of our progress, if it could be called that.

There were a number of late nineteenth century eccentrics who thought they had discovered a perpetual motion machine and were always trying to patent them, and telling the press all about their invention. I enjoyed looking into them, and sometimes you almost thought there might be something in their wild ideas. We'd put a few artists' impressions of them and their machines on our record covers. One of them was Reginald Farraway who, fortunately for him, had considerable private means as the heir of Farraway's Fennel Tea, one of those reputedly healthy concoctions that the Victorians liked to take in liberal doses. You can still get it, I think, at the back of the more antediluvian health food shops.

He had retired into the country, on the Northamptonshire and Oxfordshire border, a very quiet, out-of-the-way domain, and got on with perfecting his apparatus in a workshop at the Manor, where he lived. But he was also a most benevolent gent, and had endowed in the village The Institute, a sort of combined concert hall and reading room, a charming Arts & Crafts building with ornate lettering and flourishes, and a sprinkling of carved cogs and wheels in the plasterwork and panelling to indicate his interest. This was the best memorial to him, because he had himself left no heirs, and who knows what happened to his invention, if indeed he ever perfected it. The Manor itself was taken over during the war, like a lot of country houses.

We had sometimes hired The Institute to rehearse in, because it seemed so apt, and was good as a publicity story (not that we ever got much of that), and it wasn't all that far from where we all separately lived. It was in its own grounds, on a minor road half-way between the little village and the Hall, so our effusions didn't bother anyone. We had even given a few low-key performances there, mostly attended by the folk club crowd, who didn't, I think, get quite what they expected. Anyway, it seemed the obvious venue to rendezvous at again, as it was still convenient for us all, and we had an affection for the place.

It was good to see them both again, I admit. I never seemed quite complete without them. Triff still had her long, long hair, though there were glints of silver in it now, and her fingers were just as deft on the astral flute she had invented, while Mix still peered at us cheerily over his half-moon glasses and coaxed uncanny sounds out of a box of tricks full of protruding wires like tentacles. We'd each brought along the shape of pieces we wanted to try, and we seemed to meld just as well as we always had. Inevitably, after exploring all this new stuff, after we'd taken a picnic lunch break, we started talking about what we laughingly called our "Greatest Hits". And, of course, we decided to give a few a go. Some curious locals out for a walk with the dog looked in to see what we were up to and nodded and smiled vaguely. Sometimes the dogs joined in. At one point two ladies with kit bags and rolled-up mats realised it was the wrong day for the yoga class, and at another there was a rattling of cutlery from someone in the kitchen tidying up. "All goes in the mix," said Mix, beaming.

It was towards evening when we began to try out some of the opening passages of "Unknown Regions", just tentatively at first. The trans-dimensional crumhorn came into its own here and provided the deep ground for Triff's flute to dance and Mix to emit earth tremors and volcanic eruptions. It had usually been a twenty minute piece because that was the optimum length for one side of an album, and it had indeed occupied side two of ours. But in The Institute we lingered over it quite a lot, constantly returning to the rather haunting melody that weaved in and out of it. We lost all sense of time and were still playing as the diamond window panes darkened. The room grew shadowy, with deep pits of gloom, but we didn't stop to illuminate it and our fingers found their own way to what we needed. And then I heard a voice rising over our music, reciting in stately, measured tones, but in no language that I recognised. I glanced across at Mix, but it wasn't him, his lips were pursed in concentration on his buttons and dials. But I supposed he was playing a tape from one of our old performances where our unofficial fourth member, Archaeon as he called himself, which of course we shortened to Archie, had turned up unannounced and started reading what we supposed was his own poetry, or prophecy. He usually came along whenever we played at The Institute. We were easy-going and quite enjoyed it, and thought it added to the mystique. It was a nice touch by Mix, I thought, I didn't even know he had a recording of Archie, so I nodded across to him. But Mix seemed a bit distracted, and was darting glances across at me. And Triff was looking at us both, raising her eyebrows. I shrugged.

And then R. H. Asher, M.Sc. (Econ.) (St.) walked softly through the door, barely visible in the grey air. He smiled and leant gently against the wall. Outside I thought I heard other voices.

We instinctively all decided to bring the work to a close and began descending to a slow diminuendo, but the recitation, or conjuration, or whatever it was, did not drop with us and now began to soar out in ever more majestic phrases: at least that's how they sounded, though I had no idea what they meant. Mix began to switch things off, Triff faltered at the flute, I stopped the random noise generator and let the crumhorn just echo away the last notes, but despite all this the music didn't seem to stop. It got to the point, I am sure, where we were doing nothing but it was carrying on. And so was the voice. I stared across at Asher, who was listening, it seemed to me, carefully.

I heaved a great sigh and sagged a bit after all the exertion, and when I straightened up I thought I saw some of Farraway's plaster cogs and wheels whirring in the cornices and friezes and the gilt designs of them on the panels glinting brightly as if they too were in movement. I shook my head and looked again, and they were still at it. I pointed, but the others had already seen. Well, I'm afraid I laughed. Here were we, the original and only Perpetual Motion Machine Company, in a memorial to just such a machine, and for all we knew stuck in it perpetually, or at least until Asher intervened, if he wanted to, or the caretaker came in the morning. Asher in fact started forward and held up his hand, but it was too late. Triff and Mix joined in. We never had taken ourselves that seriously. The laughter may have disrupted things, because the voice faltered. And in among the polished oak panels, I thought I saw a face I recognised. It glimmered for a moment: the long brow and the wild hair, now white, of Archaeon.

Mr. Asher turned on the lights.

"That was him," was all he said.

Then he added: "We'll need you to try that again, soon. We want full production."

"Private gig?" I replied. "Modest fees."

"I'm sure we can cover all reasonable expenses," he replied drily.

We had never known Archie's real name, as we told him: we hardly ever used our own. People just dropped in, and, well, dropped out in those days. Asher would not say too much more, but he had to explain things a bit further before we would agree. I gathered that Archie had worked "up at the Manor" (the place had been kept on after the war), and that he—or "they"—were quite interested in Farraway's experiments, and had carried them on further. Until one day Archie had vanished. His rooms were as austere and discreet as they were meant to be when you worked there, except for the note about me. Which naturally made them wonder. And it made me wonder, too. Had Archie had a yearning for the old days? Or was he caught up in something that reminded him of "Unknown Regions"? What Asher didn't say, but I rather gathered, was that Reginald Farraway's Perpetual Motion Machine wasn't just a mechanical contrivance: it explored, shall we say, other dimensions. Lost estates indeed.

The End of Alpha Street

The left shoe must always be slightly in front of the right shoe, by just the tip. When you put them away, I mean. I don't know why, but it is so, he told me, looking at me rather furtively from his grey eyes like crystallised rainwater. Well what would happen, I said, if you evened them up, or put the right one further ahead? He turned away, took a sip of his dark ale, and stared at the white-faced clock. I don't know, he muttered, but I don't like to think about it. Then he went on, Things would befall me. I am sure of it. I see, I said, but don't things befall you anyway? What difference would it make? No, but Other Things, he said. And that was about as far as I could get him to go on that occasion, which I didn't think was too bad really. I turned the conversation away, so that it didn't look as if I was too interested.

It all began with a book called *Microethnomethodology*. I liked the title because it sounded complicated and serious, and so I would carry it around with me and read it noticeably, on the bus or in a café or even on a park bench. It was only an old battered paperback with a white glossy cover and the title in black capitals with an image of a magnifying glass hovering over some of the letters, in a rather banal interpretation of the title. The book had got more dishevelled from when I found it, by being in my coat pocket among the dust and fluff and biscuit crumbs and copper coins, or by picking up tea stains and cigarette ash from where I read it in cafés. Also it had tucked inside it bus tickets, little tawny rectangular strips, printed in smudged blue ink.

No-one ever in fact came up to me to ask what it was about or why I was reading it, but I liked to think that some at least, and those perhaps the most interesting ones, might have noticed it, and therefore me, but said nothing out of politeness. Because in those days, and I still have not quite shaken off the idea now, I thought that people must be looking at me and wondering about me. This wasn't because I thought I was especially interesting, it was more a form of apprehension, as if I might at any moment have to account for my behaviour or even my thoughts. One effect of this was that I always tried to behave politely and considerately to everyone, and on the occasions when I slightly failed to do this I would go over and over in my mind what had gone wrong and be full of remorse.

Why I proceeded on the assumption that anyone might be thinking about me was because I myself noticed and thought quite a lot about other people encountered by chance, or what we like to think of as chance. I did this partly out of a longing for the mysterious and the unusual. I hoped that some of the people might be really interesting individuals, which meant artists, eccentrics, visionaries, that sort of thing. And you could never tell, I knew even then, which of them might be one or more of those things. Certainly, their surface might suggest hints: a quaint way of speech, a flourish in the clothing, but this was not always so, and it might be that those who were inconspicuous actually harboured secret depths. I was inconspicuous, and I did like to think I might have such depths.

The book was anyway quite interesting. It was about a form of social study in which instead of looking at big significant movements, the scholar examined the minutiae of society. For example, one of the essays was about how people conducted phone calls, complete with a transcript of several. It wasn't the content that was studied, it was the way the dialogue went on, including the beginning, the pauses, the overlaps, when they spoke together or over each other, and the several false endings, when they both felt the call had served its purpose but did not want to go too abruptly.

Another survey was about the way people walked down a street, and this had diagrams which plotted out the extent to which pedestrians walked straight ahead, and when they swerved to avoid each other, and when they paused in particularly congested parts or at traffic crossings or just to stare in a shop window. The scholars who wrote these essays said that they might have practical uses, for example in telecommunications or town planning, but I am not sure they really believed this, they just hoped it might give their discipline more gravity. I think they really conducted their studies for the simple reason that they found them interesting.

I felt I might take the study off in an entirely different direction. I wondered why the focus was so much on social aspects, and not on how we each make sense of things individually, to ourselves, using our own private methods and rituals. Following this train of thought, I began to wonder about personal taboos, omens and talismans.

It was while I was sitting in the Old Cat café, which was named after an ancient tabby that used to laze in the window all the time, watching people pass by and regarding customers who came through the door with disdain. I was also watching people through the smeary window. They were trying, in a nonchalant, I'm-not-really-superstitious sort of way, not to walk under a ladder which was propped up against a haberdashery shop opposite. A man in white overalls was painting the woodwork on the second floor. Or else they were walking under it defiantly, some of them no doubt with their fingers furtively crossed. Then I had my idea. And this was to develop a version of microethnomethodology about people's highly private lore.

As with its social studies counterpart, this would not concern itself with the grand well-known aspects of folklore, such as Robin Hood, giants, witches, King Arthur, dragons, or stones that walk down to the river or the pub to have a drink when they hear the church clock strike midnight (which they never do hear since stones do not have ears, or at least not our sort of ears, so the story is really a sort of riddle or joke). Instead, I would concentrate on the really minor and unregarded bits of personal lore, the customs and superstitions that individuals accumulate and cannot quite shake off even if they like to think they are quite rational people.

I began to imagine myself as the first Professor of Personal Lore at a distinguished university, lauded in reference books as the founder of the field. I was then only a post-graduate in sociology at the Poly, and to be frank even any form of Microethnomethodology was disdained by the panjandrums there, but that didn't stop me having aspirations.

The first question was how to get people to talk about their private superstitions. And I decided that a direct question would not get results, in fact it would put people on their guard. The trick would be to first chat about taboos that a lot of people know about and perhaps follow, such as the not walking under ladders one, or not stepping on the cracks of paving stones, or not having thirteen at table, or not whistling at sea, that kind of thing. They would not mind, I supposed, admitting to something that was quite well known, as it would not seem odd, and they could even be worldly and indulgent or scoffing about them. The next step might be to admit to a piece of obscure lore of my own, which I could make up, so as not to really reveal anything, and put it forward as if I thought it was more widely known. Then when they shook their head about this I might say, well, of course there are local variations aren't there, and this might induce them to scratch around for something equally rare because there is often an element of competitiveness in conversations, as I have noticed. And this exchange of superstitions might then proceed by slow degrees to a revelation of some belief or some custom that was really quite individual to them, and then I could express wonder and praise and so beguile them into saying more.

The next question was where to conduct my field-work, as I already began to think of it, and I liked the idea of finding a small well-defined area and really concentrating on that: and after a lot of thought I alighted upon Alpha Street, the unoriginal name given by an educated developer in Edwardian times who had expected, perhaps, to go through the Greek alphabet to the end. But the Boer War had intervened and so he had yielded to patriotic feeling instead, so that Alpha Street was in fact near Mafeking Road and Ladysmith Avenue and Baden-Powell Square and Buller Mews. It was, however, also different to these in another way, in that Alpha Street was a dead end terrace with only paving stones, not a road, and it led just to a high brick wall, beyond which was a waste paper depot.

At the other, open end of the street was the highest lamppost I ever saw, which was supposed to cast light all the way along but in fact only reached about three quarters down, so that at night the further end was always in shadow. There were thirteen houses in Alpha Street, seven on the left side as you walked in and six on the right, because what would have been the fourteenth house was instead a corner pub, The Last, which hardly anybody ever went in. It was called The Last because this was a shoemaking town and its sign depicted the iron device on which cobblers shaped or repaired shoes. Others however said it was really called this because it was the last pub you would ever choose to go in, in the town, as it was so dreary.

I wondered if I would discover any differences between the private lore of the people at the open and lighter end of the street which gave out, as it were, to the rest of the world: and those at the darker end who lived beneath the high wall and within the influence of the waste paper depot, where words and pictures were compressed and baled and twined and made ready to become something else, as these words no doubt will be, sooner or later.

However, neither the pub nor the number of houses was behind my choice of Alpha Street exactly, but it was because I already half-knew someone who lived there, who I met sometimes in the public library. We had once or twice got talking about this and that, and I had subsequently stopped off at his house there for him to lend me something he thought I might find interesting. I had also, when I returned it, had a cup of tea with him there, and two arrowroot biscuits from a jubilee commemorative tin, in the front room, which he called the Sun Room, because it got the sun in the morning and early afternoon. As we talked on for a bit, we also had a glass of ginger wine which he poured from a green bottle. There were in the room plastic daffodils in a blue jug painted with a heron, and white lace antimacassars on the backs of the two red plush armchairs where we sat. The sun gave these things a quiet radiance, I thought. Although I could not exactly say he was a friend, he certainly he might be called an acquaintance.

This Mr. Frobisher worked as a clerk in one of the shoe factories but he was very keen on broadening his mind and that was why he was often in the library. He usually wore a shiny grey suit, a claret coloured sleeveless jumper, a soft-collared checked shirt and a moss-coloured tie. Claret was one of the colours favoured by the county cricket team (the other was gold) but although he followed conscientiously their scores in the paper I do not think this was why his jumper was claret. Anyway, I thought I would make him my first study.

It took more coaxing than I expected, but I did in the end get the confession from Mr. Frobisher that I reported above, about putting away his shoes with the left tip slightly ahead. On a later visit, when we repaired to The Last, he also went on to say that he wore his clothes in a strict sequence. This was not so that they all got even wear, or so that he would always be seen to be wearing fresh clothes each day, or any other practical reason. No: it was so that none of the items of clothing would feel left out. That was how he explained it to me. He did not want to seem to favour one over the others, or to neglect one. It was clear to me from the way he said this that he thought they had feelings, that they would know, and might think they had been slighted. It seemed to be a sort of animist belief. After that, however, he became quite wary of my interest and when we met he only spoke about the cricket score or interesting books at the library.

However, by then I had also got to know Mrs. Meredith, who lived next door to him. I called round when I knew he wouldn't be in, which gave me an excuse to knock on her door and ask when he might be back, and soon I was invited in for a cup of tea. This was in the kitchen because the Best Room, which is what she called her front room, was hardly ever used though it was kept spick and span. It had a picture of Windsor Castle, a three-quarters full decanter of sherry on the sideboard, and a parlour piano that I never heard played. I could see these from the window onto Alpha Street and I thought they were like a shop display, as if Mrs. Meredith was advertising Respectability.

But she was not in the least stuffy herself. Mrs. Meredith was much easier to get talking than her neighbour had been. The main thing I learned from her was that when she put the washing out on the line she had to match the colour of the pegs to the colour of the garment. She had a basket full of all different coloured plastic pegs for this purpose: but, as she explained, nobody made black pegs, so if the piece of laundry was black she allowed herself to use plain wooden ones instead. I suggested she could paint these black, but she seemed to think this was a funny idea, and said "Go On With You", with a chuckle.

Her other personal superstition was that after you had poured the hot water into the teapot you had to swill it round three times, moving the pot vigorously in a circle. This was, she explained, to get the full flavour out of the leaves. I thought there might be something in that, but I wondered why it had to be , as it always was with her, exactly three times and not two, or four, or more, and always anti-clockwise . I asked her what would happen if she put the wrong colour peg on the line and she said it wouldn't much matter if it was accidental, like, but if it was deliberate, Everything Would Be Upset. So the laundry gods are forgiving of inadvertence, I thought, but not of arrogance.

Both Mr. Frobisher and Mrs. Meredith lived towards the middle of Alpha Street and so I wanted to find out next about the personal lore of someone at the top and bottom of it. By haunting The Last a few times I got to know a cat that occasionally wandered in and leapt on one of the red velvet bar stools to demand attention. It was a lovely tawny colour and the barmaid said it came in quite often from the house opposite. "It's an English Red," she said, "a rare breed, they say." You couldn't exactly call the coat red, I thought, but sometimes when the cat was basking in the sunlight coming in through the windows, with their engravings of the brewery emblem of a white star, you could see a sort of gingery tinge. One day the cat followed me out, no doubt considering it had not quite had its full due of attention, and I saw my chance. I went up to the door of its house and knocked.

A young woman answered. Your cat is following me to get some fuss, I said, and I didn't want her to get lost if she decided to follow me all the way home. They tell me she lives here? And the cat obligingly rubbed up against my legs as if to give evidence in my favour. Oh Cinnamon! she replied, addressing the cat, are you being a nuisance? What a nice name, I said, and I see why you chose it, doesn't she have lovely colours. She is an English Red, she said, just as I expected, and with some pride, but then she went on more diffidently, of course they aren't really red exactly but that's what they call them. I thought it best to leave it at that on our first encounter but then I got into the habit of walking the cat across on other occasions, not all that often, but just enough to strike up a chatty sort of acquaintance. You have to be patient in the investigation of Private Lore: and after several such doorstep conversations, I found myself invited in.

I wondered what sort of private rituals the young woman with the cat would have and how I might find out what they were. She had given me a glass of lemonade and a couple of fig rolls and as I sipped and nibbled I said some people think cats bring luck, others the reverse, and were there any stories about the English Reds. This proved to be a good start because there were. They were supposed to be one of the oldest breeds in England, she explained, in fact some people thought they had come over with the Romans or even, and this she said hesitantly, as if unsure whether I would understand, earlier, with Phoenician tin traders on voyages to Cornwall and the South West Coast. I have heard that legend, I said (and I had), and I think it's quite possible. The tin miners in Cornwall, I went on, have some queer legends and they might well come from very ancient sources.

Do you think she knows she has such a proud pedigree? I asked, looking at the cat, which had curled up in an armchair. In fact, I learned that the young woman called her front room The Cat's Room because the feline had taken full command of it and slept where she wanted. I expect she does, she replied indulgently, and do you know I always call her Cinnamon in full and never a pet name such as Cindy or Mona because it would not do. Well, what would happen if you did, I asked, thinking I was getting nearer my goal. Oh, I am sure she would give me such a look, she said, I should quail and never do it again. Very wise, I replied, we all have our superstitions and I think we should listen to them. At this the young woman cocked her head to one side and looked at me through the long lank strands of hair that fell over her gaze, and became thoughtful. For example, I said, if I put odd socks on by mistake I always leave them on, I don't know why, and I stretched out my legs to demonstrate that I was wearing one of bottle green and another of navy blue. She laughed gently and then asked, but why can't you change them? Just because, I said lightly, just because. Don't you have similar ideas?

I suppose I do, she said. And I waited. Even though her house was at the top of the road nearest the traffic it was still quiet inside her front room with only a murmur coming through, and it was restful and pleasant to be there. There was a shelf of shabby old books, an impressionistic painting of a cat done in curves of mauve and grey, and a delicate fern like a model in green lace. It was so poised I thought it might be listening. Such as? I ventured. There was another pause. Well, you know, vaguely, and a wave of the hand (I liked the gesture). Then, I always count the stairs when I walk up or down them, she at last confessed, don't you? There are thirteen here, she added. Always thirteen? I asked facetiously. Always thirteen, she said, with a smile, then added, so far anyway. And if you didn't count them? I asked. There was another pause. Well then, I couldn't be sure they were all there, could I, she said wryly. Thirteen, I said, is my lucky number because it is the number of letters in my name, which I then told her, and thus also found out that her name was Alice.

But if you found the fourteenth stair? I bantered on. Well then I wouldn't be here, I suppose, she countered, this time swiftly. We laughed together then, but I thought that we had shared something mysterious. Did you start counting stairs when you were young? I asked. Yes, that might be it, to see how many I could climb, perhaps, she agreed. I thought I ought to stop there as I didn't want to undo the magic of her stair-counting ritual, so I rose to go. You are quite inquisitive, you know, she commented, as she saw me to the door. I was on the verge of confessing that I was a folklore student, but instead I said, only with people I find interesting, and I could see that was the right thing to say, although there was also a look across her face that suggested she wasn't quite fooled by such talk. It so happens that I continued to call upon her, accompanied by her cat Cinnamon, even after I had got the lore I wanted.

The houses right at the end of Alpha Street were the two darkest because the streetlight, as I have explained, never got that far and because they were under a high wall. The one on the right never seemed inhabited, at least I did not see anyone about there. But the other one looked like it was. I thought about asking one of the other residents, Mr. Frobisher, Mrs. Meredith, or Alice, about who lived there, but I decided that would make them dubious about why I wanted to know. I wasn't quite sure for a while how to strike up an acquaintance with the occupant, but at last I decided on a simple ruse. I waited until the early evening and then walked purposefully to the brick wall and looked bewildered (this was all play-acting in case I was being watched, as I always thought I was). Then I turned cautiously to the left and made looking, searching sort of motions. There was a narrow side passage leading to the back yard and I ventured into this. In the yard I saw a thin stooped figure, bending down and straightening up again repeatedly. He did not seem to hear my approach but as he turned in my direction I saw he had a sheaf of scrap papers in his hand. I supposed they must have blown over from the depot and he was tidying up.

Sorry, I said, I thought there must be a gate so I could cut through. But it's a dead end is it? Yes, he replied, it's a dead end. You can't get through. Must be a nuisance, I suggested, nodding at the paper. He looked at it too, as if this idea was new to him. Do you get a lot of it? I asked. When it's windy, I expect, I added. He did not respond to this. Could you tell me how I get round? He hesitated then. It occurred to me that he had never needed to find the way round or might have only the vaguest idea how to do so. Often we know the least about the things nearest at hand. We stood in silence in the dim light. He shuffled the paper about. It might be best, he said, if I try to draw you a map. It's not straightforward. You can't just go through, you see. I see, I said, that would be very kind, if it's not too much trouble.

When he ushered me into his bare front room I was taken aback. There was only a table and two hard chairs on the cold flagged floor and the rest of it was occupied by stacked wooden crates, which all, so far as I could see, were full of paper like the sort he held in his hand. In fact, he put this latest gathering carefully on top of one. I'll have to get a piece of paper, he said, and I sniggered, thinking this was a little joke. But he went off out of the room and came back carrying a used manila envelope. You don't like to use these then, I said, gesturing to the crates, do they come and collect them from you, up at the depot? I thought maybe he had an exaggerated sense of other people's property and kept them in case they should ask for them back, even though they were only scrap. Nobody comes for them, he said, no, but I don't like to, and then he tailed off. I read them, he said, what the wind brings. You never know. There's a lot to read. Oh, I replied, a bit at a loss. Then, I expect you might get all sorts of interesting things. He nodded. I picked up a few pieces, idly, and I saw him watching me closely, but he didn't try to stop me. I glanced at them quickly

One of them was a fragment from a football pools form, showing some teams from the Scottish Second Division: Queen of the South, Stenhousemuir, Brechin City.

Another was part of a street plan, showing curving, squirming roads with blurred names, Regency Avenue,

Restormel Road, The Triangle; and a third was what looked like a knitting pattern for a cable-wear pullover in an old mustard colour. Then there were some thin, tissuey sheets of bible paper, with smeared text, which I have since learned was from the Book of Habakkuk, and there I read, and remembered, Woe unto him that saith to the wood, Awake; to the dumb stone, Arise. These I read aloud, I don't know why. And the words rang hollow against the walls. For a few moments it seemed to me as if I had in fact said to the wood of the crates, awake, and to the stone of the floor-slabs and the walls, arise, and as if they very well might. As if they were thinking about it. And I had a picture of all these sheets of paper, soiled, crumpled, tainted, flying over the wall to land in this man's yard as if they were bringing messages to him, or so it might seem. To each of them, I reasoned, whatever was written on them, their message was of urgent importance, for this was the word they had been made to say, no matter what it was, and they were determined to bring it.

The stooped figure moved forward now and gently took the pieces from out of my hand and placed them carefully back where they had come from. There are quite often things like that, he said, as if he were making an excuse for them. But I read them all, he went on, I read them all, whatever they say, whatever the wind blows my way. You never know, you see, he said, you never know. No, I said, you don't know. Then I left. He never did make me the map, and so I have never found the way through.

The Fifth Moon

The Ninth Legion, the Princes in the Tower, Fair Rosamund, Robin Hood, King Arthur and William Rufus had already been taken, so I thought for a bit and suggested King John's Treasure, and Hambledon said this was quite a good idea as treasure always attracts interest and readers also like villains. I said I thought John might have been a bit hard done by in history and he said that was another possible angle, if I wanted to paint him a bit differently.

And so after some lively conversation about terms, I was signed up to produce in a couple of months a volume for Hambledon's "Mysteries of History", a scheme of which he was quite proud. There must be a map for the endpapers, he said, they're all having maps, that's another thing people like. I said I could manage that all right and in any case it would be necessary, because the coast had moved a lot since King John's day and where the treasure was, if there was any treasure, was now some miles inland.

Then, while he was still in a good mood, I said I would need a photographer and he should find a bit more in the kitty for him, and the man I had in mind was John Rook. I saw Hambledon struggling to swallow this extra outlay, and so I said that it would get a few more sales because Rook's work had a certain following due to his uncanny ability to capture moods, in fact I said, you might be surprised that even more people will want his pictures than those who want my refulgent prose. In the end we agreed I'd chop a bit off my fees towards this cost, and he'd put in another bit. So I wrote at once and gave the good news to Rook.

The idea behind Hambledon's series was that as well as exploring the historical mystery each book would also be about the local landscape, and indeed I knew he had the notion of covering the entire country in this way if he could find enough mysteries. I had the hope that if this one turned out all right we might get a few more from him and so have enough to keep us going for a year or two, which we certainly needed. Because, despite what I had said to Hambledon, patrons of literature and the arts were sometimes surprisingly chary about stumping up even sufficient funds to keep us in tea, beer, bread and cheese, to say nothing of cigarettes and such incidentals as a bed and a roof and blankets and firewood.

I had remembered about King John because once at college, our tutor, in desperation, poor fellow, had given us each to read a copy of a paper, from *Archaeologia*, which he said would show us what history really could be: original, ingenious and even exciting. I remember I was polite, but inwardly sceptical. However, I soon found he was quite right. It was W. St. John Hope's essay on the loss of the King's baggage train in the Wash.

This paper had made it all quite enthralling. The old historian had looked into every detail. He had calculated the times of the tides for the exact day in question. He had also worked out, from contemporary accounts, how long the baggage train would be, and therefore how long it would take to cross the treacherous sands. He showed how the medieval coast could still be traced inland along the line of what is now called the Roman Bank. There was even a chart, showing the sort of terrain where the treasure must be (and this I thought I could draw upon for Hambledon's endpapers). He did not know *exactly* where it must be, of course, although plenty of others thought they knew, or said they did, but he had narrowed down the region fairly precisely. And after reading St. John Hope, I had felt I could quite picture the scene. I remember I looked up from his quarto pages, and it was as if I could hear the east wind wailing over the saltmarsh, could witness the panic of the men and the horses, could imagine the terrible rush and roar of the waves, and almost see the gleaming jewels and shining swords and rich regalia seized by the sea, never (so far) to return.

There was another excellent reason for me to choose this particular mystery, however. I knew Stainton, the painter, had a former wildfowler's houseboat, beached out there on the marshes, and as he was often away I thought he would probably let us borrow it for a few weeks for next to nothing. I'd visited him there once or twice and even rashly bought a painting from him when I was temporarily in funds: it was a local scene, a sonata in murky grey and sallow green which certainly seemed to capture all the desolation and loneliness of the place. The boat was ramshackle, draughty and devoid of almost all comforts, but it would do for two to live in for a few weeks and would save us having to stump up for a hotel or inn, and that would make Hambledon's largesse go quite a bit further.

It was moored, or rather marooned, not far from the old sea bank that St. John Hope had written about, and also, just as importantly, only a couple of miles from a fairly decent pub, which we could easily reach of an evening, provided we minded our steps on the way back. Because, as I found out one night when Stainton and I had stayed on a bit too late and drank a bit too long at the inn, it is all too easy there to get lost in the marshes, and they are still treacherous. It was only because I had remembered to bring a torch and the painter had left a lantern out on the awning of the boat that we were able to find our way back. Otherwise we might as well have been walking in one of his great grey-white empty canvases, doomed to wander forever in a world of nothing. A map, indeed, I thought would be needed: a careful, hand-drawn, very detailed map. I would make that one of my first tasks.

And so after I had written to Rook, I wrote also to Stainton care of the *Bittern* (his boat), Foul Anchor, Cross Keys, via King's Lynn, and asked if we might have the vessel and if so could he send me a map of how to get to it (for I did not quite trust myself to remember this) and mark on it places of interest thereabouts. I also explained what we were up to, and asked him about anyone on the scene we should go and see about the story. Because that was another aspect of the series that Hambledon was quite keen on: you needed to introduce a few experts, preferably with quaint ideas, who would reveal local lore overlooked until now, or at least not in the weightier histories, so that readers thought they were being let in on secrets. Well, I knew there would be no shortage of people who had notions about the treasure, and I hoped Stainton could give me a few hints about where to find them.

A few days later I received a characteristically brief reply from Rook, in his spiky handwriting like black railings, agreeing to the plan and thanking me for getting him in on it. This was followed after a few more days by Stainton's crumpled and spattered sheet of paper saying he was himself about to go and paint in a disused beacon tower on the coast of Pembrokeshire, and we could take care of the *Bittern* for a month or two and send him anything we could spare whenever we could spare it. On the back of the sheet was a rudimentary map showing a railway station, the boat and two pubs, with the note "only places of interest". There were also two smudged asterisks, and arrows leading below, where, distinctly as an afterthought, were two addresses, and the words; "Try these. But don't blame me . . . "

Inside the envelope were two enclosures, equally bent-about and paint-speckled. One was the card, printed in neat black lettering in a Roman type, of a Major R. H. Tanderlane FRGS, The Saltings, with his postal and telegraphic address. On the back of it Stainton had scribbled "Friend of mine". The other was a leaflet, folded in half, advertising a lecture some months past by Dr. E. Drage, on "The Truth Behind the Treasure". Stainton had added, "Find her at the marshland museum."

We took the rattling train in a third class smoker on the Midland and Great Northern Line, which Stainton had told me was known locally from its initials as the Muddle & Go Nowhere. Rook's bony face, almost axe-like in its sharp edges, was softened by the wraiths of tobacco fumes emanating like silver genies from our cheap cigarettes. Through this haze could be glimpsed, under the black flop of hair on his forehead, his pale blue eyes, which I sometimes thought regarded every scene they ever saw as if sizing up what it would look like caught in a rectangle in black and white. On the other journeys we had done together, both the few commissions and the expeditions we had made on our own account, speculatively, I had begun to admire the way in which he noticed contrasts and compositions. Working with him was like seeing the world presented at another angle. There was a quality of attentiveness in him, a sort of gentle, inheld calm, which was as much a part of his art as the camera itself and the tireless work in the dark room later.

Sometimes, however, I have to admit, it was inconvenient to linger around quite so long as he liked to do. In the early days of our association, I used to urge him to "run a few off" so we could move on to the next stop, a phrase which he accepted with a stolid, silent reproach. I soon learned there was no hurrying him, and if I grew restless while he waited for the light to change or the shadows to move, I would wander off looking for anything else of interest. Often enough, too, around a corner or along some unpromising side-street, I would then encounter some oddity or feature worth describing. So we soon settled into a way of working that suited us both.

After we had passed terrain increasingly dimmed and lonely, we shuddered to a halt at the little wayside station of Walpole. We shouldered our few bags and got out. On the desolate platform there was a one-storey waiting room and ticket office, with a sort of pointed pediment above the door, and next to this the station master's house, four-square, red-brick, with a tiled roof, about as standard a habitation as one could expect to find. But something about it caught Rook's attention. Another thing about him is his unwavering courtesy in the matter of photographs. He will devote some time to finding the correct person and asking for permission before he takes a picture. This invariably leads to conversations, which are seldom short. People tell you all about the thing you are looking at, then tell you about the photographs they have themselves taken. It's true they are usually pleased to be asked, but, what is not quite so helpful, they often assume they are to be part of the image, or else why would we be asking? Rook doesn't like to disappoint them, so he takes a few without them, "to get the light right, you know" and then one with them, which rarely gets used. Sometimes, however, either the pose or the character of the individual will make him think the piece worth preserving.

The station master at Walpole had seen to the tickets of the few other passengers, waved and whistled the train away, and then turned to us as we loitered politely until we could get his attention. Rook asked if he might photograph the platform and the buildings, and, after the "trial" shots, the station-master stood watchfully and solemnly in front of these while he did so. I have a print of that picture in front of me now, and I suppose I can see why Rook wanted to take it. There is something caught in time there, some poignant aspect to the way the old man stands there proudly in his peaked cap and waistcoat, the flag aligned to the edge of his trousers, a spot of black light glinting from each burnished boot, and the last of the pale steam from the departing train still lingering on the platform. Years from now, that moment will still exist while all of us, Rook, me, the station-master, will have gone.

"On holiday, are you, or here for the fruit-picking?" he asked. Evidently he could not quite place us. Our voices, I suppose, our manner perhaps, suggested one thing: our patched jackets and scuffed shoes (and third-class tickets) another.

"Sort of holiday," I said. "Staying over at Foul Anchor. On an old boat. Is it far?"

Stainton's map had omitted any scale and I vaguely remembered something of a walk. The station-master's worn face, which put me in mind of some salt-eaten ship's figureheads I had once seen in the museum at King's Lynn, cleared. Now he was able to place us.

"Artists, I see," he said. We did not disabuse him: well, we were both artists, each of our kind, even if not with paints. And he gave us careful but largely incomprehensible directions of the sort that turn out to be very useful once you know the way, depending as they do upon knowing the names of the various unmarked local lanes, and who lives in which house. We did at least glean that it might be thought "a tidy step" but "not so badly" for young gentlemen (there was the faintest hesitation here before he gallantly gave us the benefit of the doubt) like ourselves. He pointed out the start of our way, which even I could have worked out, since it was the only road heading east, towards the (far distant and stoutly deterred) sea, and leant on the furled level crossing gate to see us go.

As soon as we set out in the chill air of early October we caught the sweet, slightly over-blown smell of ripe apples and on either side of the lane were walled orchards. The silvery, crusted bark of the trees glimmered in the dimming light and they held up their twisted branches like antlers. For a moment it was as if we looked at columns of statues depicting ancient horned gods. The track was well-rutted from the carts taking the sacks of the first pickings to the big dark Dutch barns. The sun behind us was low in the sky and muted by drab clouds.

In a few minutes we came to a fork in the road, and I took a hesitant right. We were now at the little hamlet of Cross Keys, which consisted of a few brick terraces of fruit-pickers' and water-workers' cottages, and other houses at odd intervals, each with a temporary, flung-together sort of look about them. Even the post office was in a kind of chalet with a corrugated iron roof, almost a shed. The whole place looked huddled up against the empty level plain that stretched beyond it to the east. Apart from a couple of boys busy on their ancient bicycles, there was no-one about.

After a short stroll we came to the inn, which also bore the name of Cross Keys. I pointed to its painted sign.

"One key unlocks the door to heaven and one key the door to hell. According to the local tale, anyway."

"Put it in the book," said Rook, but he gazed up at the emblem critically. "And yet both keys look the same. How would we know which door we were opening?"

"Not the door to the beer, anyway," I replied, for the pub's arched oak entrance, studded with black nails, was firmly shut. Still too early, it seemed, despite the lowering light.

Rook looked around at the wan country beyond. I could see him eyeing the scene with all his usual appreciation of the bleak and austere and, since I wanted to get to the *Bittern* while we still had enough light, I tried to divert him with talk of the place.

"We'll be coming back here a lot," I said hastily, "it's the nearest settlement to us. Also, if the old historian is right, it's on the very verge of where the treasure might be. The old sea bank, you see, that existed in John's day, curves around just beyond here. This was the last safe place before the causeway across the Wash and into Lincolnshire."

Rook looked at me from under his dark flop of hair, not fooled by my diversionary tactic.

"All right," he said. "So all that"—he gestured to the land ahead of us—"was under the sea then?"

"At high tide, certainly," I replied. "Otherwise it was an estuary of creeks and saltmarshes. And of course mud. Sucking mud," I added, with some relish.

"And yet it looks like settled land now. How long has it been drained?"

"Less than a hundred years," I said. "The new embankment is much farther out, and there are miles of reclaimed land before you get to it. The boat, thankfully, is on the nearer edge of all that, just beyond the old bank. But Stainton took me further out there a few times. I don't mind telling you I found it a bit—well, unsettling. Since it's all new land there's obviously nothing old there at all. It makes you realise how much we take for granted the familiar signs of human use that normally lie all around us. But out there it's as if someone has taken a rough cloth and wiped clean every trace of us."

"Not such a bad idea," observed Rook mordantly, "and, no doubt of it, some potential for the cold eye of the camera."

"Ye-es," I replied, a bit reluctantly. It wasn't a terrain I had any great desire to enter again. "We could get a few mood pictures, perhaps. We wouldn't need to go very far for those. You know the kind of thing. 'Where these rich ploughed fields now stretch to the horizon was once the raging sea.' "

Rook nodded. "And is there really nothing very much at all?" he asked, a little too eagerly for my liking.

"Well, there are drainage channels," I said, hoping this might dampen his interest. I should have known better. Far from it.

"Yes, I expect so," he said. "Very interesting. I like lines leading to the horizon. Lots of opportunities for perspective. Semi-abstracts, you know. That kind of thing."

But I could see by the slightly teasing look in his eyes that he was only half-serious. Still, I wouldn't put it past him to spend an entire day on the drainage channels. I had known him to spend at least as long on a line of telegraph poles stretching over downs, or breakwaters on a shoreline.

"It isn't quite deserted, of course," I said. "There's a couple of farmhouses, I seem to remember. And Stainton says they built some observation posts there during the war. Oh, and there's an old tin mission hut. They put it up for the navvies building the new embankment and doing the draining. I expect they'd have preferred a pub. It's a long walk to the nearest. It's a little museum now, all about the drainages. We might head for it if we do go out that way."

"Yes," said Rook, and I could tell that I had only excited his interest further. "Tin, rust, salt. What could be better? There should be some fine effects."

"There speaks a man satisfied with the simple things," I replied, "Not for you the crowns and jewels of this world. But don't forget that's what we're really here for. Out there," I pointed somewhat vaguely north, "if the tales be true, lies the most fabulous hoard ever known. That's our mystery. Is it there or isn't it? And why hasn't any of it ever surfaced?"

"Spirited away, if it ever did, I should think," said Rook. "This doesn't strike me as what you might call 'telling' country. They keep things pretty close here, I imagine."

"Spirits, indeed, from what I hear," I said. "Also lace from the Low Countries. There was a lively trade in contraband, that's for sure. Shouldn't wonder if some of that still goes on. I don't think we'll enquire too much in that direction. But now, I'm not quite sure which road we take here."

We had come to the meeting of five ways. There was a black and white signpost, which offered us Terrington St. Clements ahead, and, confusingly, also at an angle to the left, and Shepherds' Gate to the right. The arm pointing to the sharper left turn simply said "The Marshes". Rook took out a silver pocket compass with a dented lid. He flipped this open and the green needle pointed back the way we had come.

"It's the marshes for us," he said, "at least that's the road due east. 'For lust of knowing what should not be known, we take the Golden Road to Samarkand', and so on."

The road was not all that golden. Some faint shafts of sunlight did gild its brown puddles, and some of the stalks of grass on either side had faded to a sort of tired yellow. There were no longer any orchards, nor trees of any kind except one tall sentinel poplar, which had already lost some leaves to the sea winds. We fell into silence as we trudged along this cold lane, which seemed to act like a funnel for a bitter rush of bleak salt wind. It was a relief to come to another junction, and here I recognised a landmark from my previous visits. Ahead was a long low hummock of rank grass, overgrown with black-green nettles, the ghosts of dandelions and a few bristly purple thistles.

"The Roman Bank," I said. Rook turned behind us to look towards the lingering strands of low, veiled sunlight, and then back to study the abandoned embankment. I tried to see the old earthen sea barrier as he did, and waited while he crouched low so that he could capture the way it loomed out of the land like a great green serpent. When at length he was done, I led us through a gap in the bank along a dank track that led away from it, and lengthened my stride towards the boat.

There was ten minutes more walking before it hove into view. It was difficult to miss. For one thing it was the only immediate object of any upper dimension that rose up from the reclaimed land. But Stainton had also ensured it could easily be found by painting it in great streaks of scarlet and gold, so that it looked rather like a wooden sunset. The word "Bittern" was inscribed along its side in bold characters of black. By the side of the track were the crumbling remains of an old stone quay, still with rusting mooring rings in deep corroded tints of pink and copper.

Next to this was the boat, although it might be better to say what once had been a boat. What remained, as a sort of platform, were the prows and deck, and there was also the compact narrow cabin with its gloomy looking windows. But there were now no masts, and next to the cabin, either Stainton or its previous owner had constructed, from wooden panels, a sort of ramshackle extension, stretching out towards the stern, so that the living quarters were made longer. At the bow end, an awning had been erected, of stout canvas, now streaked with damp green. The whole structure, part boat, part shanty, leant at a slight angle against the derelict quay.

We went rather unsteadily on board and dropped our bags onto the deck, which seemed to bear our load soundly enough. The old cabin had been converted into a sort of galley, with a black round-bellied stove from which a chimney had been tilted up through the roof. To the side of the stove, Stainton had obligingly left a small stack of logs and some brittle brushwood for kindling. There was a folding table and a couple of wooden chairs. On the table a handwritten note, held in place by an iron candlestick adorned with congealed white tears, said: "Help yourself to the stores. Top them up when you go."

We examined Stainton's idea of stores. They consisted of half a bottle of whisky, four bruised apples (undoubtedly windfalls), a tin of condensed milk, a jar of livid yellow piccalilli, a battered tin with a portrait of General Gordon on a camel, which proved (the tin, not the camel) to contain what we supposed must be ship's biscuits, a large bag of porridge, and a blue waxed-paper bag marked "dandelion coffee", inside which was indeed something brown and powdery. There was also a row of glass vessels of various kinds, each labelled "drinking water", not that I had often seen Stainton let water pass his lips whenever something more potent was to hand. It was just about possible to imagine some sort of bizarre feast composed of these ingredients, but clearly replenishing the stores must be amongst our earliest tasks.

We crouched under the low doorway into the saloon, as Stainton liked to call the added room. On either side of this were two narrow beds, which doubled as seating places during the day. A chest, against which we would certainly at first bark our shins, occupied part of the middle, and proved to contain blankets, oilskins, a single somewhat withered orange, and the torch. Some of Stainton's pictures were stacked with their backs towards us against the wall. There were playing cards, and a few books and maps, all dog-eared, in a little niche. A makeshift skylight let in a certain amount of illumination, and there was an oil lamp and a couple of storm lanterns. Just outside, a cracked shaving mirror on a three-legged stool, and a red watering can rigged with wire above an alcove formed by a striped folding windbreak indicated a somewhat Spartan form of ablution.

"Welcome to the Hotel Bittern," I said. "All modern conveniences. Moderate terms. Artistic appurtenances. The perfect hideaway for the modern traveller."

"Indeed it is," said Rook. I hadn't been too sure what he would make of it, but his grin and the dancing amusement in his pale blue eyes showed that he approved. "And such original cuisine. I don't know how it is, but a piccalilli and porridge potage has never yet come my way before."

The night was not restful. The bed was not only narrow but hard and I kept on almost falling out of it. The boat creaked, sometimes ominously, so that I thought, in my half-sleep, that it was about to topple over. The awning flapped, the watering can clanked, and the black stove, which we had stirred up to a decent fire, continued to make cracking and hissing noises. But besides these, which I could at least explain, there were other odd, less accountable sounds. The cries of birds were plaintive and seemed always to carry a brittle echo, the wind, though it was by no means yet high or strong, found holes to whistle through, and the dry reeds whispered with their sad salt tongues. I knew, or hoped, that I should get used to all these in time, might even come to welcome them, but for that first night onboard they were, to say the least, disconcerting. The remedy, I thought, would be some staunch walking to make me tired enough not to notice, and my prescription also included the opiate effects of either Stainton's whisky or the inn's beer, should we ever find it open.

When morning at last came in its grey stealthy way, therefore, I suggested to Rook that our first plan was to walk as near as we could the exact route of the King's baggage train, from the outer edge of Cross Keys, over the county boundary into Lincolnshire, and so to Sutton, which had in those days been the point of landfall after the estuary had been crossed.

"In the footsteps of the King," said Rook. "Chapter title."

"Thanks," I replied, "But alas not so. On the trail of the treasure, perhaps. The King wasn't with it."

As I explained to Rook, while we enjoyed our cigarettes at dawn, John had arrived at King's Lynn, then called Bishop's Lynn, during his campaign of plunder against the lands of the barons who opposed him. He had been warmly received: the town supported him in his wars with the magnates. Then his entourage divided in two. He and his mounted soldiers, many of them mercenaries, took the surer but longer road west to Wisbech, while the much slower baggage train, of packhorses and carts, took the short cut across the estuary. This was passable for a few hours at low tide, led by a guide who knew the sands, who walked ahead with a long staff to test the firmness of the terrain. But, and here stories differ, either his household did not wait for the guide, or they proceeded against the guide's advice. Some of the sands were still treacherous: probably the leading carts got stuck. The safe passage was narrow: those behind could not go round the obstacle. The passage also depended upon moving swiftly, so that the sands could not take a hold, but as the whole procession came to a halt, boots and hooves and wheels began to sink slowly but inexorably into the salty mire.

Rook nodded, and began to polish the lens of his camera, his most precious possession. It was a Cyclops, hand-made in small numbers by a firm in Wiltshire. It was more compact and sturdier than most instruments and, according to Rook, a poem in black and chrome. He treated it like a sacred vessel.

After a scratch breakfast, we retraced our journey back to the little railway hamlet, passing some of the apple-picking crews already busy about their work on short, tapering ladders propped against the old trees. They seemed to be mostly young women, nearly all dressed in overalls and headscarves, except for one who wore a black beret at a jaunty angle over dark hair that curved around her ears and nape: a workmate said something to her, and she turned to regard us as we passed. There were also a few old men in caps, mostly giving unnecessary instructions in a hoarse bawling, and a scamper of young boys picking up the fruit that fell. At the end of the settlement was a large Georgian house with tall, glinting windows and walls of grey stucco, guarded by high cedars, and a grove of ash and beech. A fair-haired young man in a high-necked scarlet pullover was sweeping and raking the leaves, and nodded as we passed.

Just beyond this I pointed to our left, where a great grassy bank swerved away: this was a continuation of the Roman bank, curving round from where we had encountered it on our way to the boat, and it marked the edge of the safe land in medieval times, and indeed for some centuries afterwards. The railway now cut straight through it, on its way to Sutton: indeed the road ahead accompanied the line all the way there.

We stopped to gaze to the right of the railway and the road, out over the Wingland Marsh, the new land wrested from the sea barely a hundred years since. The ploughed fields looked rich in their deep brown furrows. There were hardly any houses or barns to break the long plains of loam. The brittle blue sky was marked by the slow flap of a few birds—a heron, some gulls, crows, some over-wintering geese—and their coats of old blue, ice white, black and silver were a momentary relief from the low dark land. They were like heralds passing through the heavens announcing the coming of minor angels.

"Somewhere out there," I said, keen to break the silence that the scene had seemed to impose upon us, "is where the baggage train foundered, at least by most reckonings. There are other theories, of course. Like Avalon and Camelot, it ever glimmers elsewhere."

"Oh," said Rook, "I didn't know Hambledon was paying you for poetry as well as honest prose."

"If it had got into difficulties close to the bank, where we are now," I continued, ignoring this chaff, "then it could have just turned back, or at any rate more might have been saved. And similarly, if it was close to the end of the track across the sands, then presumably more would have scrambled ashore. And so, it is assumed that it must have been overtaken by the tide when it was more or less out in the middle."

We looked again at the long brown fields, trying to imagine them covered with the roaring sea. I wondered what the plough sometimes turned up. But not so much as a buckle or a coin or a piece of harness had ever emerged, at least so far as the official histories knew.

Then I turned to look in the opposite direction, still beyond the old bank.

"On the other hand," I said, pointing now to the left of the railway and road, "some people think the crossing was made rather lower down, over what is now known as Walpole Marsh."

The view was very similar, except that there were rather more houses to see, and, welcome to the eye, more mature trees, finely tinted escutcheons of crimson, copper and gold. Their deep, ancient colours were a rich delight after the chilly paleness of the fens and the skies. This part of the country had been drained earlier than the Wingland Marsh, and had a distinctly more settled look to it.

Despite the old romance that seemingly lay all about us on either side, it was a dull trudge along the straight road between the two rival terrains, and even Rook's keen interest in simplicity and long lines did not lead him to stop often. It was a relief when we came to the Victorian swing bridge, with its little turret, at Sutton, and crossed the great murky channel of the Nene. We paused in the settlement that had grown up around the bridge, and had cups of tea in a café with steamed-up windows.

When we returned, the doors of the Cross Keys were still closed, so we carried on into Terrington St. Clements and bought some more supplies to supplement Stainton's somewhat erratic selection. After we had carried them back to the boat, we had a lunch of bread and cheese and real coffee, even risking some of the phosphorescent piccalilli by way of garnish, and a couple of apples. Then we lit our cigarettes and tilted back our chairs on their hind legs for greater contemplation.

"What's next?" asked Rook.

"Next," I said, "I think we shall make a call upon one of Stainton's friends. Let's see." I looked at his scribbled addresses and the asterisks marking where they were. "Major Tanderlane. He's not far away. Might as well find out what we can. Besides, Hambledon likes to have a few 'local characters' woven into the story. Human interest, you know. And you can do a flattering portrait of him looking wise in the half-light."

The house called The Saltings had its back to the marshes and set its gaze resolutely towards the west. Its orange bricks seemed to have captured years of the dying rays of many sunsets. At the gateway two pillars each held a stone globe, like blank heads. The garden was guarded by a tall, thick holly hedge, a wall of spiked tongues. In the middle of the shaggy lawn was a crumbling grey urn from which dead creepers drooped. At the door, tall monkshood flaunted its purple banners. There was an off-white push-bell in a panel of brass corroded with a pale green crust, and a door-knocker of some figure involving horns. I pressed the bell. A dull peal like an old gong sounded inside.

A tall, lean figure, with skin like parchment and a long face notable for its dark, arched eyebrows, and deep-set brown eyes, came to the door. He wore a peppery tweed jacket and a rust-red woollen tie, tucked into a mustard-yellow waistcoat.

"Major Tanderlane?" I enquired. "Our friend Stainton gave us your name. The painter, you know. We're staying in his house-boat for a bit."

He said merely: "Stainton? I see. Yes," and ushered us in. The entrance hall, though quite a large room, seemed to contain only an umbrella stand, a hat rack and a lofty grandfather clock, whose face held, as well as the main timepiece, a complicated circle of minor dials. What their delicate hands measured, or indicated, was not immediately clear, but there was a painted moon and several radiant stars.

"Come through to the study," he said, and gestured us to seats upholstered in a faded green velvet, with curved, claw-footed legs. We looked furtively around. By contrast, this room was stuffed with things. Lamps and candlesticks were placed on every available surface. Sheets of foolscap paper, some furled up, others held down by stones and pebbles, were filled with rows of minute blue-black manuscript. Piles of books seemed to be held in a complicated and almost impossible balance by the side of chairs and tables, as if those on the top were waiting only the correct moment to leap away. There was a great chart affixed to the wall: it seemed to consist mostly of sea, and the ermine markings denoting marshes. One octagonal side-table only was kept almost clear: on this resided a gleaming tantalus. Our host approached this and, with something of the manner of an acolyte at Mass, carefully took out three glasses, unstoppered a bottle and then turned to us, as one who faces the congregation.

"Malmsey?" he asked. We assented. The tawny liquid slithered into the glasses, and he handed one to each of us, then, with the merest slight tilting of his own glass, but without any words, made a gesture as if in some private form of benediction.

"About the treasure," he said, and there was a slight inflection that made the remark almost a question. The long pause afterwards also gave this impression, so I hastened to fill the silence.

"Yes. Stainton kindly suggested we should call upon you. I asked him who knew most about it, you see."

"But you do not, I hope, expect to find it? Nobody ever has."

"Oh, no, not at all. No, I'm more interested in the stories told about it. Legends and so on. And, well, Rook here is a photographer, working with me."

He looked from one to the other of us.

"Stories, yes. Well, where shall we begin?"

To my surprise, Rook cut in at that point.

"One thing I should like to get clear, sir," he said, respectfully, "is what exactly the treasure was. It must have been important to have caused so much stir. But do we know just what was lost?"

He seemed gratified by this question.

"Yes, indeed, we do. In fact, a very formidable lady wrote about that not so long ago. What was her name now? Saw her lecture about it. Jenkinson. That was it. A. V. Jenkinson. Never did get her first names. We weren't quite on those terms, d'you see? Might have been Audrey, I suppose. Or Ann. Or . . . "

I thought it better to forestall any further recitation of female names beginning with A.

"And she had found out about what the treasure was?" I prompted.

"Mmm? Oh. Yes. Quite. In fact, she was surprised that no-one else had tried to answer just that point. It was all there, in the papers of the royal household. The, what d'ye call them? Court Rolls. Paper Rolls. Patent Rolls! Yes. That's it."

He held up a single amber-hued long finger. "One thing that must be said for King John, you know, is that he put the affairs of the kingdom in good order after the neglect of his feckless brother Richard. He devoted a lot of time and attention to administration. But no-one ever achieved a reputation that way. History prefers the lionhearts. Did a bit of soldiering out that way myself, in fact. With Allenby. Palestine. The Near East. Funny how we keep poking our noses in there. However . . . "

He took a few sips of his Malmsey and leant keenly forward.

"What she said was, that John had been gathering all his treasures together, from their places of safe keeping with abbots and priors, castellans, and the masters of the Knights Templar and Hospitaller. Everything that was returned to him was listed by his clerks, and that's how we know what he had, and so, presumably, what was lost. Certainly much of it is never heard of again. I have made it the object of my special study, you see. There were hundreds of precious items. Crowns, swords, caskets, gem-stones, even jewelled staves. What he wanted with those I couldn't say. Symbol of office perhaps. Waft them about to impress his courtiers."

He made a gesture with his arm, in illustration, nearly upsetting a tall candle-stick of twisted iron, and the white taper within it.

"There were, for example, the Rings of Innocent, a gift from the Pope. Four rings, of emerald, sapphire, garnet, and topaz. They each had a symbolic meaning, as the Pope explained to him, though what those were I don't think we now know. Then there was the Sword of Tristram, with its broken blade, a most ancient talisman. There was also, most probably, the Imperial Crown of the Empress Matilda, from her marriage to the Holy Roman Emperor. And something called the Wand of Gold, a holy sceptre I gather, made of rose-gold, a wonder to behold. But these are simply the pinnacles of his treasury. The sheer amount he gathered together is quite incredible. People talk about Tutankhamun's tomb, you know—"

He glared at us from out of the arched tunnels of his eyes, as if up till now we had been freely chattering about the young pharaoh.

"Lot of stuff there, I gather. But this. It's no wonder the barons got a bit uppity with him, if he flaunted it all. Enough to make a saint peevish, I should think. Here, I made a note from the list she read out. Let me see now."

He reached for one of his scrolls of foolscap and peered at it.

"Green Boy. Witches' Broth. True Ivy. Devil's Candlesticks. Black Medick. Hmm. No, that's something else. Wondered where I'd put that. No. Now, what about this? Yes, here we are."

He cleared his throat, held the paper out in front of him, and raised his head as if about to make a proclamation.

"One hundred and forty three cups, mostly white silver. Fourteen goblets, eight flagons, forty belts of leather or silk, studded with jewels, fifty-two rings, sixteen staves, two candelabra, two thuribles, half a dozen caskets, and three golden phylacteries."

Something about the manner of the Major's recitation made me want to add, "half a pound of tuppeny rice, half a pound of treacle," but I restrained myself.

"Just to take the staves alone," he continued, "they were decorated with rubies, sapphires, diamonds, emeralds, garnets, topazes, and bloodstone. And that, mind you, is only some of it."

A distant look came into the Major's brown eyes, as if he were imagining the shining hoard he had described. Then he put the sheet of foolscap aside, and tugged at the folds of his ochreous waistcoat to straighten it.

"But all that is of no importance, you know, once you grasp the real message."

I took up my cue. "What is the real message, sir?"

He drummed his fingers on the arm of his chair, then looked at us both sharply in turn.

"Was it ever lost at all? Is it still hidden somewhere else entirely? Or was it all stolen by his mercenaries when he died, just a few days later? Well, what I ask myself is this. Who started the story that it was lost in the Wash? Two monkish chroniclers, that's who. Were they just covering up for someone, or telling a pious tale about what happens when you lust after riches? Maybe it was just meant to be a moral fable."

I nodded. "Yes, I can see how that might be so. The medieval way of thinking must have been very different to ours."

He frowned. "But that's not all. What does the story mean? Don't you think it is all one grand allegory, eh? This drowning of the treasure? All those jewelled wonders sunk in the slime. That brilliant light dimmed by the ooze, worn and corroded by the grey waves. Those noble instruments taken forever from their high task. Just so are we, certainly, once gleaming spirits, sucked down into the dull clay of our bodies, and trapped in the dark decay of matter."

He hesitated once more, clearly unsure of how much to tell us.

"There's a lot of talk out here about what happened to the treasure. You'll hear some tales if you ask around. Treachery in the king's household, for one. Kept safe by the Templars, for another. And then, later on, rumours that the secret has always been known, by the smugglers, or the sand-guides, or the embankment-keepers. I'll tell you, some of these are just a bit of local wit, as they like to think. They take a pride in jossing the outsiders. You sift them all, these tales, and see what you think. But as for me—"

He sighed, and took a last sip from his glass.

"I picked up a certain amount of, ahmm, knowledge out East, you know. Met a few chaps in Alexandria. To the initiate, I suggest, each of those jewels represents a trapped soul. And I am convinced that all these stories of the loss of the King's treasure conceal a truth which is of profit to us all. Not worldly profit, of course. Spiritual profit, of signal importance to our souls. If we ever found even the merest gem-stone out in those marshes, then it might be a sign that our return to the light was at hand. But we never have. And I fear we never shall."

He shook his head, and lapsed into a sorrowful silence. Outside in the hollow hall the grandfather clock sounded the hour with a deep timbre that was almost a groan.

I thought it was our opportunity to go.

"Very good of you to give us this original and profound insight into the story," I said, shaking the Major's lean, worn hand.

"Friend of Stainton's, pleasure," he murmured. Then his expression lightened a little. "Did he tell you to go and see the old girl out in the marshes? Ah, thought he might. Yes, well, she has a completely different view of the matter. I don't say she's wrong either. Something in it. Worth a listen, anyway."

He accompanied us to the door, where he stood among the purple monkshood. Rook asked if he might take a photograph of him. He at once adopted a stiff pose, as if he was still on parade. As we walked to the gate, and looked back, we saw the old gnostic raise a hand in brief farewell. When we passed below the stone orbs on the top of the gate posts I half-expected them to swivel around to watch us go. In the distance I thought I caught sight of the boy in the scarlet jumper cycling nonchalantly away on some errand, with no hold on the handlebars, hands in the pockets of his breeches.

As we walked back through the village, I noticed a dark opening in the door to the Cross Keys. It was at last open, it seemed. A quick suggestion to Rook, and the motion to adjourn was carried *nem con*. We entered a narrow flagged passageway. One door to the left was closed but another on the other side stood open. It gave onto a small parlour. On the wall there was a coat rack, calendar, clock and a photograph of fields under water: the flood depicted also lapped at the edges of the main street we had just traversed. Rook studied it briefly.

There was a narrow serving hatch for a counter, and a brass hand-bell. I gave this a cautious shake. There were footsteps and a woman appeared, wearing a lavender-coloured house coat. She waited in silence. I asked what there was in the casks, and she mentioned three beers, in a firm, take-it-or-leave-it sort of tone. All three were not at all bad, and I took back to our table two pints of dark porter. In the dim light of the room it gave out glints as if it concealed black rubies within.

We both looked around at the rest of what I suppose must be called the "snug", although it didn't exactly live up to the name. There was a bench along one wall, a narrow, unlit fireplace, one long trestle table and a cluster of smaller, square, two-legged ones. There might be space for about twenty customers, if they didn't mind each other's company. But just now there were only two others in, a girl with cropped hair the colour of damp bark, and an elderly man with vigorously-combed white hair and a long, sharp nose. Their heads were bent over a game of dominoes. They seemed very intent on the play.

Rook and I found ourselves, as one does in the presence of strangers, talking in lowered tones. We lit cigarettes, and the fumes stole stealthily across the room.

"Well," said the photographer, "did you get enough 'local colour' from Major Tanderlane?"

"Colour, certainly. Local, perhaps not. I don't think he's from here. But he asked some sensible questions, even if his conclusions are a bit . . . "

I trailed off, partly because I wasn't quite sure what I wanted to say, but also because I had sensed the slightest movement from the other table. But when I glanced across at them, the two still seemed absorbed in their game.

"I'd like to try the out-marshes tomorrow, beyond the boat," Rook murmured. "The camera needs horizons."

"All right," I said. "I'll see if I can find this Dr. Drage at the museum. But we'll try to be back at the boat by dusk for a feast of whisky and ship's biscuits."

After a bit more discussion of our plans, Rook gestured to our glasses.

"Just a half," I said, "it's a touch rich on top of that Malmsey . . . "

While he went to the hatch, I stood up to study the flood photograph again. As I turned back, I glanced down at the other table. Something caught my attention. I noticed that the markings on the black tablets they were solemnly placing were not the usual white dots, but pale stars: I could make out their pointed white rays. At first I thought this must be just some flourish of a particular maker. But then I saw that the stars were not arranged in the same form as the numbers generally are in dominoes, such as two columns of three for the six, or a quincunx for the five. Instead they formed shapes that looked like the maps of constellations. So far as I could, without staring too hard, I tried to work out how the pieces had been placed. They did not seem to match each other, like the standard way of pairing up the same numbers, but were put into position by some other system of scoring evidently known to the players.

I shifted my gaze from the pieces on the table to what I could see in the players' hands. This would be bad form under any circumstances, I admit, and I became at once aware of the young woman snagging my stare. I smiled, and stammered an apology.

"Sorry—I haven't seen that game before," I said. "What's it called?"

She looked at me from out of dark eyes. The white-haired man ignored me.

"Dominoes," she said.

"Oh, yes, I know that, of course. But I've never seen it played quite like that."

She shrugged. "It's the way we've always played it."

I nodded, and rejoined Rook as he returned with the drinks. He had overheard some of the brief conversation, but a look between us showed a shared understanding not to discuss it. The two players continued as if there had been no interruption. We did not linger much longer. Our murmured conversation about the rest of our plans was conducted to the steady rap of the star-form dominoes slotting into their place, whatever that was.

In the morning we walked east from the *Bittern* along the narrow track. It ran in a straight line to a thin belt of trees, silhouetted against the pale sun. Wherever I gazed were muted colours of bleached green and faded grey, as if nothing had enough sap or bloom to achieve any deeper hues, and even these pale tints of sage and ash seemed to falter one into another. In the leached October day, the thin clouds gave no relief to the eyes: they were like tatty, dirty net curtains drawn in rags across the horizon. The tracks that joined our road were also dead straight. On the map they formed long rectangles like deed-boxes, and as we passed them they all looked alike. They were narrow, often pockmarked with stagnant pools, with a ditch on either side that held a dribble of tarnished water. Tussocks of stiff, determined grass clutched at the verges. Rook stopped us a few times to take pictures of the pools and ruts in the road, black holes and slits that seemed to hold a glinting darkness. Once we came across the last vestiges of another marooned boat: its rotting wood had begun to form an alliance with the mud. At intervals there were footbridges of only a few paces in span: they seemed to lead from nowhere to nowhere. All around us was a brittle silence.

It was a relief to catch sight of the tin mission hut, on a slight rise, perhaps a bank formed out of a spoil heap. Next to it were a few crumbling brick outbuildings. It had once been painted green, but much of that had been scoured away by the salt winds, and there were streaks of rust. A small bell-canopy was perched on top, and as we drew nearer we heard the sound of its thin desultory peal whenever the sea breeze caught it. A black and white sign announced that this was the marshland museum, curator Dr. E. Drage MA, FRSA, and a faded piece of paper advised that she was in attendance most days from 10 AM, and outside these hours the key was under a brick by the door. I retrieved it and let myself in, while Rook, with undisguised delight, started to photograph the corroded tin walls, and the views from the little elevation on which we stood.

The museum was neatly organised. In one corner was a desk and there were display cabinets with finds from the reclamations and a brief history of the work. A diagram showed each phase of the embankments through history, starting with the "Roman" bank we had seen and then all the others through the ages, like ripples of human effort against the sea. That the ancient battle was not all one way was indicated by pictures of inundations and shipwrecks. Some rather hazy photographs showed groups of wary labourers, with caps and knotted neckerchiefs, standing outside the mission church. A note said that after the church was closed it had been decided to commemorate their labour and dedication by turning it into this small museum, funded by the drainage companies and voluntary subscription. In obedience to this tactful nudge, I put a few coins in the collection box. To one side there was a bookcase and a map chest, and I began to riffle through the contents. I liked being in this little sanctuary from the bare land beyond: it seemed to restore a human touch, to hold within it a sort of quiet defiance. It showed the signs of care and respect for the past. I settled myself on one of a few wooden chairs that looked left over from the former church, and began to read some of the books and learned papers. Often as I looked up to think about what I had just read, I could see Rook prowling around, his spare body stark against the pale sky.

I was so absorbed by my researches and note-taking that when the door opened I did not at first turn to greet the figure that emerged. Then I was aware of a presence looming over me. I looked up to see a weather-beaten face from which little black eyes like burnt currants peered.

A dry voice said: "Drage." She was dressed in a stout tweed coat and corduroy trousers. I introduced myself and Rook, who had followed her in, and explained our work.

"Most interesting," she replied. "Be sure to mention us in your book. We welcome, as you see, visitors. I will be with you in a moment." She busied herself with tasks in what was evidently a well-practised routine, then settled proprietorially behind the desk. "Draw up a pew," she said, gesturing in front of her. We both brought chairs. She sighed, and gazed out of the window for a few moments, then turned her dark stare back to us.

"Lot of nonsense talked about the treasure," she began. "Though he was no saint, there's no doubt King John has been wronged by history. In sober fact, the inglorious episodes of his reign were all due to the vested interests who opposed him—the barons, the princes of the church, the rivals to his throne. Stop me if I get borin', by the way. Bit of a hobby horse of mine." She chuckled to herself: the noise was like water gurgling down a drain.

"Y'see, one of the best pieces of advice for any historian is this: always go back to the earliest sources. That is what I have done. There are only really two contemporary accounts of the loss in the Wash. The one that is most often quoted is by Roger of Wendover, a credulous man who reports as fact all sorts of rumours and gossip. If you want monsters and marvels, he's your man. Should we trust him? Not a bit of it. Well, it is he who says that many precious vessels and treasures were lost. The other account is by Ralph of Coggeshall. Now he is a careful and factual man. And what does he say?"

She leant forward in her chair and looked at us keenly.

" '*Capellam suam cum suis reliquiis.*' "

I struggled to construe this. Dr. Drage, like my former teachers, was quick to discern my difficulty.

"Ha! In plain English what he says is that King John lost his *chapel*, with all his relics. Yes, there were also some household effects: '*supellectilis*', you know, ordinary things, furnishings if you like. That was what was in the baggage train. Not a word about crowns and jewels, you see. King John's treasure, if we believe Ralph, and I do, was *not* a worldly one. It was a *holy* treasure. That was the loss he lamented most of all. He was a devout collector of sacred relics, you see, many very rare. And a superstitious man. He understood this grievous loss as a sign that the saints and angels had deserted him. Smoke?"

She offered us a box of thin cigarettes in black paper. We each took one. She struck a match and as I leant forward the light seemed to glimmer in her dark eyes. The strong fumes caught at my throat.

"From the mountains of Lebanon," she said. I thought at first she was citing some biblical text, but she gestured at the cigarette box. "Won't have anything else."

"Where was I? Ah, yes. Well, now all those relics are buried, we must suppose, somewhere out in the marshes. Really, that makes the land around what was the estuary the biggest reliquary in Britain. The most sanctified place in England, not even excepting perhaps Canterbury or Glastonbury."

"But surely all these tales . . . " I put in.

"Are simply what people wanted to believe. They prefer Roger's story to Ralph's. More fun, ain't it? How much more thrilling the idea of lost crowns and swords, and jewels and gold coins. And indeed there may have been *some* precious caskets and chalices and thuribles, as part of the chapel. But it *was* a chapel that was lost, and not the contents of a palace. As I say, go back to the sources, and weigh them up."

I could see that contrasting the two tales could form a useful counterpoint in the book, provided I didn't quite disparage the richer story as much as Dr. Drage did. Somehow, as she noted, saints' bones, however holy, didn't have quite the same allure as the sumptuous list Major Tanderlane had recited. Hesitantly, I mentioned this detailed catalogue from the Patent Rolls. She snorted.

"All that tells us is what he had. Not what he lost. Yes, yes, a lot of it seems to disappear. Not surprising. The country was in chaos, you know. Civil war. The Dauphin was in Kent, hopin' to bag the throne himself. When John died, his own mercenaries and followers were seen carting off booty quite brazenly. He'd probably already used much of it to keep 'em with him. No mystery there."

Rook delicately extinguished his black cigarette in the ashtray.

"What are the local stories about the treasure?" he asked, quietly.

"Interesting," said Dr. Drage. "I think it suited the local people here to foster the idea of a golden treasure. It's said that it has always increased the price of the land, just because of the chance of finding something. And certainly there's been a flow of parties coming here looking for it. Treasure means treasure-hunters. They bring in money, too, you see: they rent cottages, stay at the inns, employ local people, and so on.

"I can tell you this, though. The families most linked to the story don't say anything unless they want to. I tried to interest them in the museum. They were generous in giving me exhibits—but not stories. I tried to speak to the ones who used to know the marshes and keep up the embankments, but they were remarkably tight-lipped. You'll know the marsh families by their local names— Salvage, Delamore, Thurlow, Neap, Malward. The current generation are beginning to leave the marsh and go further afield, but some of the children always seem to remain here and carry things on."

"And so there might be something there after all?" I prompted. For the first time the curator hesitated.

"They like it to be *thought* that there is a secret, and that they know something. But whether there is . . . "

She shrugged.

I spent some more time with the museum's archives, while Rook photographed Dr. Drage herself, and the exhibits. As she had said, I encountered frequently the names of the local families in the various stories told about the treasure: one were descendants of the sand-guides who had led travellers across the marshy estuary; others were long-standing keepers of the embankments, responsible for their repair and maintenance; there were also water-fowlers, eel-fishers, farmers and fruit-growers, all from lineages settled here for centuries. I compiled hasty notes of as many of the anecdotes about the country and its great mystery as I could.

On the walk back, I reflected on the curator's brisk account of the historical sources. It seemed eminently sensible. Yet it was hard to regard the terrain we trod as holy ground, sanctified by the lost relics. There was no sense of ancient sanctity here. I felt instead that there was something else I could not quite grasp, beneath the surface in every sense. There was an inheld, brooding quality to the land, and I did not want to linger out in these farther marshes as the day drew on. The blazing sunset paint of the boat was a welcome sight as we made our return.

Later, seated next to the fat stove, I spread out a map on my lap and began to think about all the material I had gathered from the notes in the museum. The crackling of the fire and the creaking of the boat made a sort of lulling refrain to my studies. I turned over my pages of notes, and plotted out in my thoughts the journey over the saltmarshes, consulting the map to trace the various routes suggested. There were about half-a-dozen local traditions I had jotted down, but they all seemed to cluster around the old marshes, among the first to be captured from the sea, that we had seen when we had stood at the edge of the little hamlet of Cross Keys, by the Georgian house with its cedars, and grove of ash and beech.

I seemed to drift into a gentle trance and my fingers loosened their grip on the map. In a haze between waking and drowsing, I rehearsed in a stream of images the country we had walked in, the people we had seen, and the stories and theories we had heard or I had read. The shifting of a log in the fire, like the sudden furtive movement of a wild animal, tugged me back to full awareness. I blinked, sighed, and reached for my cigarettes, then returned my attention to the map. As my gaze hovered over it, my attention was caught by a name I had not noticed before: The Hollow. It didn't seem to be a house or a monument: the italics suggested some natural feature, and an unusual one in this level landscape, which had so few contours. I looked at it carefully and then at the country that lay around it.

To the north of it was Marsh Cottage, where one story said the hereditary bank-keepers by the side of the Nene had once dredged up some treasure. Further west was the old Tide Gate, whose smuggling families were also attributed to know about more than contraband. To the east was the outer end of Cross Keys, where the estuary had once begun, and the sand-guides lived. My gaze strayed south: yes, there was the King's Farm, another reputed source for the lost treasure, though others said it was named for a different king. It was as if all the tales formed rays around a focal point that itself was never mentioned: the heart of the star. With a lunge of understanding, I saw that the purpose of the myths must be to draw attention *away* from the place, to all the peripheries of the old marshes. Seekers would spend all their time sifting these various claims, never seeing what lay at the core of them. I lit my cigarette and smoked thoughtfully for a while.

Tomorrow, I decided, it was time to visit The Hollow. And what more suitable day? It would be the 12th of October, the anniversary of the great loss.

There was a sullen dawn. The sky wore a white mask of clouds. We breakfasted on porridge and coffee, then left the boat and walked back up the track into the hamlet and past the Cross Keys pub, shuttered up and silent. There were no fruit-pickers in the orchards, and the haggard apple trees raised their grey horns alone. We went on to the end of the settlement, where the stucco of the Georgian house seemed made of the same pallid colour as the clouds. Just beyond, at a junction, I took us down another narrow lane. It had thick hedges of hawthorn and elder on either side and it was not possible to see beyond. Ridges of grass grew in its middle. We seemed to be on it longer than I had expected, but I supposed this must be due to our steady pace. It came out at last in another tangle of roads. We could glimpse a few houses and some stands of trees, but nothing much in the way of a landmark, so we leant against a gate and consulted the map and Rook's compass. What the map said and what we could see did not quite match, try as we might to reconcile them.

We chose a road that looked closest to the one we wanted, and went slowly along it, still not quite sure of our way. Although the views were more open here, they did not disclose very much that was useful. The terrain all seemed much the same: long, tilled fields, a few others left full of scrub, thin lines of trees, and the silver glimmer of water in channels or ditches. The road seemed to take us in a long curve, unusual in this domain of straight lines. When it finally petered out, we did not seem to be any further forward, despite our walking, and scanning ahead and around, than we had been before. We retraced our steps and tried a few side-roads: they did not seem to go anywhere in particular either. And yet I was sure we could not be far from the place marked on the map.

The morning was beginning to dwindle away. We stopped and reconsidered.

"We can't expect there to be a sign to the place," I said, "it's not even clear exactly what it is. We could have passed over it on one of the roads without knowing, I suppose."

Rook nodded, but remained quiet for a few moments. Then he said: "Listen."

I did as he said. From a little distance, there was a persistent, drawn-out rushing noise, like the waves on the shore. But it could not be that: the sea had been banished from here centuries ago. The only other sound that might be like it was the wind in the trees. There was a chill freshet of air on our faces. We both gazed towards where the long sighing seemed to come from. There was nothing obvious at first, but then I caught sight of the feathery tips of trees trembling in the breeze: they had not stood out before because they were below the line of sight; they must be in a deep dip. Together they seemed indistinct, blurred, in a purple-grey mist. In contrast to the cultivated fields we had often passed, the ground between us and the trees was like moorland, left to itself. Newly encouraged, we continued following the obscure track we were on until we came to a little iron wicket gate. From it the faintest of paths could be discerned, heading over the grey-green grass towards the trees.

As we approached, the susurrus, rising and falling, rustling and soaring, seemed more than ever like the sea driving over a long reach of sand. It was not that the wind was strong: it was bitter enough to send a shiver through the limbs, but did not resist our progress through it. But it was persistent and had its own rhythm, and we followed its call. We did not at first realise we were coming upon The Hollow. The ground only gradually sloped down, until we came to the brim of a steeper drop, a scoop in the moor where a grove of birch trees had gained a root-hold. Their white bark and slender forms, and the mauve fronds of their delicate twigs, gave a gentle grace to the pit, which was clustered with dark green moss, nettles and thistles. We began to scramble down the side. By some curious effect of the deep chamber, as we descended, the sighing sound made by the trees seemed to diminish to a distant echo. But it was replaced by a heavy silence that began to bear down upon us as we dropped to the ground. There were still gleams of light here from the pale trunks of the birches, but in between the trees was a dimness. I was already making up some text to myself: "Could this remote place hold the secret to the King's treasure?" and so on, and I thought we would just stay long enough for me to form the impressions I should need to describe it later, and for Rook to get a few moody shots. There were no obvious paths, and the going underfoot was stony as we wandered through the grove.

I can't say how I first became aware of an oppressive atmosphere about the place. It seemed to steal upon me gradually. At first I thought it was just the silence, the shade and the sense of being shut off from the rest of the world. They were certainly enough to foster some unease, but it wasn't just that. I began to feel that the place possessed a darkness it was slowly releasing: I knew this could simply be the first onset of the decline of the day's light, but yet it seemed deeper than that. I kept thinking that the white of the trees and the grey in-between the trees was not quite staying still: that shapes were shivering out of them. It was probably the effect of the slight swaying at the top of the trees, but it made me even more unsure.

The curious thing was that as I looked at John Rook, who had braced himself against a tree to take a photograph of the interior of the grove, he seemed to glimmer also, and his usually sharp, austere form was blurred at the edges. I supposed this was also caused by the diminishing light, but I could not shake off the idea that some aspect of him was being dissolved. I called out to him, but he remained in the same hazy suspense. There was the briefest flicker, as if he had moved in recognition, but he did not respond. Perhaps, I thought, he is concentrating on his framing, but as I took a few steps towards him I turned my ankle on the uneven ground and fell forward. My face sank into a mingling of mud, moss and old leaf-mould, and I caught its rank odour filling my breath. Jarred and winded, it was a few moments before I could heave myself up, and then only with great labour, as if I was being pulled down.

When I did at last regain my feet, Rook had moved further into the grove and the flickering over his figure was more intense: I could barely distinguish where he ended and the darkness began. I stumbled further forward, swaying against the birch trees, glad of the crusted touch of their scaly bark: it seemed a definite thing in a world that had grown indefinite. As I followed Rook haltingly on, I glanced back: I could now scarcely make out the margins of The Hollow.

Above, the dash of the wind through the upper reaches of the birches was still causing the sweeping sound so much like the onrush of waves upon the sand and though this was subdued where we were below, it was still like an otherworldly whispering. With a determined effort I caught up with Rook and took hold of him by the shoulder, not just to stop him going any further, but also to make sure he was still fully there, so insubstantial had he seemed.

"Let's get back," I said, "we're losing the light. Didn't you hear me call?"

He looked at me hard. "I did," he said slowly, "but when I turned to look you weren't there."

"I fell," I replied.

"But then," he continued, "I thought I saw something that must be you farther in. I supposed you'd gone on while I was busy."

"That wasn't me," I said, quickly. I remember how zealous I was to deny that I was the other shadow he had seen.

We both stared ahead of us. There was nothing moving now. And yet there came over me the sense that we were among what I could only describe as a sort of active darkness. It wasn't the shade from the thin trees: if anything they still gave a quiet light from their pale limbs; and it wasn't cast by the grey pallor of the clouds. There was a dense, thriving blackness all around us that seemed to come out of the ground and out of the walls of The Hollow. I had the conviction that if we stayed much longer we would begin to merge into it, meld with its utter pitch. Already I began to feel a stealthiness entering my limbs, diffusing throughout me. I seemed to lose all sense of volition, as if I wanted to succumb. I sensed dimly that something was being stolen from me, yet I felt too hazy and dazed to deny it. I seemed to be gradually merging with the blackness that lapped in The Hollow. I think we must both have hovered there for some moments on the brink of being absorbed into this dark force. It was a small thing that caught us back: the call of a human voice. It seemed to jolt us both into ourselves again, perhaps only momentarily, but enough to make us move.

We turned, shook each other roughly, then blundered back through the trees, several times nearly tripping, sinking against the white tree trunks when we needed support, scrambling up the slopes, clutching at clumps of grasses, kicking our shoes into any toehold we could find. As we neared the top, hands reached out to us and hauled us up. I caught sight of the set faces of the younger domino-player and the boy in the scarlet jumper, before they briskly urged us on before them. We dashed along a way that we had certainly not been able to find, which seemed to lead more directly back to the hamlet, only pausing for breath as we neared the cedars guarding the Georgian house.

Inside, after we had bathed our hands and faces and brushed our clothes, we joined our hosts—and rescuers— in a drawing room illumined by a great chandelier. Its iridescent light was very welcome, and so were the leaping flames in a deep stone fireplace. But as if this was not enough light, those in the house moved around the room lighting tall white tapers. These were reflected on pale lime-wood panels which seemed to hold their glow like old lanterns.

There were four ranged before us: the white-haired man and the girl who had played dominoes with him; the fair-haired youth we had seen sweeping leaves in the grounds of this house; and the young woman with dark hair who had looked at us from the orchard when we had passed on the second day. They regarded us thoughtfully for a while. And then one of the young women stood up and recited what I at first thought of as a most peculiar passage, until I discovered its source:

> —"My lord, they say five moons were seen to-night;
> Four fixed, and the fifth did whirl about
> The other four, in wondrous motion."—

I was about to interrupt, but she held up her hand and the boy intoned:

—"Five moons?"—

And then the other young woman concluded:

—"Old men and beldams in the streets
Do prophesy upon it dangerously."—

They resumed their seats. The older man sighed, and said, in a weary voice: "King John, Act IV, Scene 2. So: you didn't believe in any of our four fixed moons, then? What we might call the embankment-keeper's tale, the smugglers' tale, the sand-guide's tale, and the farmer's tale?"

Despite our ordeal in The Hollow, I smiled at the adroitness of the allusion.

"No, I didn't. I thought I saw, as you might say, a fifth moon dancing among them."

He nodded appreciatively.

"Well, I understand that at least you have already heard the old prophets. We've been keeping an eye on you, though not quite well enough—"

He held up a hand to cut off my protest.

"For your own good, as you have just found out. Now, these two prophets. Let's give them their due, they've worked some of it out. The old Major, and all his talk of jewels and souls. That historian in the out-marsh and her idea about the chapel and the relics. There is a lot of truth in all that. But not all of it."

Although I was still somewhat overshadowed by our earlier experience, I had not lost my instinct for chasing after the story.

"And can you tell us the rest of it?" I asked. He regarded me steadily.

"Well, you found The Hollow. Not many do. It's not a good idea. Why do you think we've spread all those stories farther away from it?"

"I worked that out," I said, with, I admit, some pride. "But once I plotted the stories on the map I saw there was a gaping hole in the middle of them. So of course I had to go and look at it. I suppose I can see why you don't want people to go there. What is it?"

He responded to my question cautiously.

"It's one of the places where they took some of the earth to build the later sea-banks. There are others. That's why it's a hollow."

"Yes, I understand that. But what's there?"

"Well, when you take up soil here, you also get salt and silt and sand. The residues of the old estuary. And so of course you find things."

"What sort of things?"

"In a moment, my friend. We've been finding them for a very long time. And keeping them to ourselves. Looking after them. Oh yes, we'll tell you, since you've got so near. And you can tell it again for all you like. Because they won't believe you. It's not what they want. They want treasure. Not this."

The three younger members of the company were watching him keenly. The light showed all the strong lines on his face. They were deeply marked, and I seemed to see a burden upon him. His expression tightened.

"It wasn't a chapel that King John lost, though that's what the chronicler says. That might have been the story it suited the church to tell. We haven't found anything of it. But do you know what they said about his line? The Angevins? Descended from the devil. They used to joke about it. This King, though, must have thought it was more than a joke. Or at any rate he liked to assuage what we might call—other powers. What we found, our families, many moons ago, was this. What was lost in the sands wasn't the crown jewels, wasn't a hoard of riches, and it certainly wasn't holy. It was a sort of devil's chantry."

"A—what?" But my thoughts were already among what we had sensed, what we had glimpsed, in The Hollow.

He permitted himself a creasing of the mouth that might have passed for a smile.

"The relics we have found are not saints' bones or their bells and cups and so on. They are quite different."

I glanced across at Rook, who was listening patiently and impassively.

"But—what are they?" I said, bewildered.

He rose, and took up one of the white candles. In the corner of the room was a tall cabinet. Taking a small key from his pocket, he unlocked the glass-panelled doors, and gestured us forward, holding up the taper so that it cast light inside.

Displayed on polished wooden shelves, which in their austere simplicity and solidity had something of the air of an altar, was an array of objects. I stared at them. There was a salt-bleached curl of pale yellow wood, a great white oval pebble, a piece of dented rusted metal, a leathery black frond, and a shiny dark curved fossil.

Each of them had a label, hand written in ink with a flourish to each of the letters. I leant forward to read them. They said: A Rim from the Cup of Judas, used at the Last Supper; The Egg of the Cockatrice, as Foretold in Isaiah; A Fragment of the Horn of Israfel, Which When Gathered from the Parts of the Earth Will Sound the Last Trump; A Feather and a Claw from a Fallen Angel.

I stood there for some moments, trying at the same time to memorise the contents and to make sense of them. I also had an unsettling urge to laugh.

Our white-haired host moved the candle away, and the shadows fell upon them again. Carefully he re-locked the door. We resumed our places. I did not know what to say. It seemed like some absurd hoax, but they had been shown to us so solemnly that I felt almost convinced that they believed in them. And then, there was, after all, the darkness we had glimpsed.

The exhibition of the objects seemed to have unsettled the old man's equanimity. The brown-haired girl put a hand on his arm, reassuringly.

"You understand?" he said. "You understand? This is King John's treasure. These are the real relics that were lost. Things that were not holy, that he had worshipped beneath the mask of his devotion. And it was these that he invoked, these that received his prayers, these he expected to summon to his aid. These were the things whose loss he so lamented. These—and other things that I cannot show you. Those we returned to the sea."

I felt I had to get this clear. I was still suspicious that this was some elaborate jest.

"But—they look just like things you could find on any shore after the tide has gone," I protested. "Driftwood, a pebble, dried seaweed, shells, rusty metal. They can't be what you say they are. How do you know?"

He turned a darkened gaze upon me.

"We know because The Hollow tells us. Unlike you, we do not go there unprepared. For centuries we have listened, and gathered up whatever it yields. To keep it safe. But have it your own way. Perhaps they aren't what the labels say. They could be just our disguise for something else, couldn't they? And what would that be, do you think?

But you won't ever know, will you? Our families found out the truth years ago, and we have guarded it ever since. And we know how to use it, too, when we have to."

He had said all this in a level voice, as if conceding a point in a courteous learned debate. But yet there was the very slightest hint of a threat in his final remark. And I remembered what the Major had said about how hard it was to know if the inhabitants were exercising a dry wit, and what the curator had said about them always wanting to leave the impression of a still further secret. I tried one more sally.

"Do you know," I remarked, also, I hoped, in a gentle tone, "I think the fifth moon is dancing still."

But he was not to be drawn, and it was clear I would not be given the opportunity to press further: the last word had been said.

Our host stood up in a definite sign that the discussion was at an end. We were ushered courteously but firmly to the door. They watched us go down the drive, past the great cedars, and out into the hamlet. Dusk was already gathering upon the road. We strode out strongly, both keen to be back on the boat before the darkness came upon us.

Sources

"A Chess Game at Michaelmas" was first published in *The Pale Illuminations*, edited by Robert Morgan (Neuilly-le-Ventin: Sarob Press, 2019).

"Fortunes Told: Fresh Samphire" was first published in *Grotesqueries: A Tribute to the Tales of L. A. Lewis*, edited by Jonas Plöger and Mark Valentine (Düsseldorf: Zagava, 2022).

"The House of Flame" was first published in *Sorcery & Sanctity: A Homage to Arthur Machen*, edited by Daniel Corrick and Mark Samuels (Brighton: Hieroglyphic Press, 2013).

"The Seventh Card" was first published in *Supernatural Tales 42*, edited by David Longhorn (Winter 2019/20).

"And maybe the parakeet was correct" was first published in *Supernatural Tales 45*, edited by David Longhorn (Winter 2020/21).

"The Readers of the Sands" was first published in *Crooked Houses*, edited by Mark Beech (Egaeus Press, 2020).

"The End of Alpha Street" was first published in *Strange Tales: Tartarus at 30*, edited by Rosalie Parker (Coverdale: Tartarus Press, 2020).

"The Fifth Moon" was first published in *From Ancient Ravens*, edited by Robert Morgan (Neuilly-le-Ventin: Sarob Press, 2017).

"Worse Things Than Serpents", "Laughter Ever After", "The Understanding of the Signs", and "Lost Estates" are previously unpublished.

Acknowledgements

My grateful thanks to the editors and publishers of the books and journals where some of these stories first appeared, as shown under "Sources".

I owe the Thomas Hardy reference used for the title of "Worse Things Than Serpents" to Philip Wilkinson at his *English Buildings* blog.

About the Author

Mark Valentine is originally from Northampton but now lives in Yorkshire near the Leeds-Liverpool canal. He likes second-hand bookshops, vegan food, overgrown gardens, stationery shops and village hall flea markets. As well as his fiction, his other books include studies of Arthur Machen and Sarban, and four volumes of essays on book-collecting.

SWAN RIVER PRESS

Founded in 2003, Swan River Press is an independent publishing company, based in Dublin, Ireland, dedicated to gothic, supernatural, and fantastic literature. We specialise in limited edition hardbacks, publishing fiction from around the world with an emphasis on Ireland's contributions to the genre.

www.swanriverpress.ie

"While small publishers often produce beautiful books, few can match those from Swan River Press."

– Washington Post

"It [is] often down to small, independent, specialist presses to keep the candle of horror fiction flickering . . ."

– The Irish Times

"Swan River Press—cutting edge of New Gothic."

– Joyce Carol Oates

"The redoubtable Brian J. Showers [keeps] the myriad voices of Irish fantasy alive there in Dublin."

– Alan Moore

SELECTED STORIES

Mark Valentine

In St. Petersburg, amidst an uneasy truce with the revolution, there exists a secret trade in looted ikons. But who are the dark strangers seeking for the Gate of the Archangel? In the small town of Tzern, news arrives of the death of the Emperor; meanwhile a postmaster, a priest, a prophet and a war-wearied soldier watch the dawn for signs of the future. Constantinople: A quest for the lost faiths of the former Ottoman Empire leads a French scholar to believe that the strangest may also be the truest. On the edges of Europe, exiles and idealists meet in a café to talk of their hopes—while sinister forces begin to march. These stories, exquisitely told by Mark Valentine, are about individuals caught up in the endings of old empires—and of what comes next.

"Dense, allusive, and thoroughly satisfying."

– Dead Reckonings

"[These stories] are all imbued with a strangeness and beauty that takes them—and the reader— several removes from what is called realism."

– Supernatural Tales

"Valentine is a master at capturing the ineffable in prose."

– The Agony Column

SEVENTEEN STORIES

Mark Valentine

Mark Valentine's stories have been described by critic Rick Kleffel as "consistently amazing and inexplicably beautiful". He has been called "A superb writer, among the leading practitioners of classic supernatural fiction" by Michael Dirda of the *Washington Post*, and his work is regularly chosen for year's best and other anthologies.

This selection offers previously uncollected or hard to find tales in the finest traditions of the strange and fantastic. As well as tributes to the masters of the field, Valentine provides his own original and otherworldly visions, with what Supernatural Tales has called "the author's trademark erudition" in "unusual byways of history, folklore and general scholarship". Opening a book will never seem quite the same again after encountering this curious volume of *Seventeen Stories . . .*

*"Valentine is a writer in love with
the great tradition of the weird tale."*

– Supernatural Tales

*"[Valentine's] is attentive to place and to the power of
obsession, but one of his true gifts is an ability
to suggest modes of artistic expression."*

– The Endless Bookshelf

A FLOWERING WOUND

John Howard

Two of the stories in this collection by John Howard have their setting in a certain west London suburb—the calm prospect of its small houses and tree-lined roads is deceptive. And throughout this selection of stories, whether in outer London or hyperinflationary Berlin, Romania in the febrile 1930s, or the austerity Britain of recent years, we encounter people who live on the peripheries of their cities and societies—and at the edge of their own lives and illusions. They might think they know the rules, but it often turns out they do not, after all. Or perhaps the rules changed—silently, abruptly. In these stories past and present come together with wounding consequences for those caught out by the system—or its absence.

"Some stories recall Arthur Machen's approach
to London, his insistence that the great metropolis
is a place of magic and mystery."

– Supernatural Tales

"Full of haunting stories of love and confusion . . .
a very suitable accompaniment to these terrifying times."

– A Ghostly Company